BURN

Jennifer Natalya Fink

suspect thoughts press
www.suspectthoughts.com

This book is a work of fiction. Names, characters, places, and incidents are either products of the author's imagination or are used fictitiously. Any resemblance to actual events, locales, or persons, either living or dead, is entirely coincidental.

Cover image and design by Shane Luitjens/Torquere Creative.
Book design by Greg Wharton/Suspect Thoughts Press.
Author Photo by Frances Sorensen.

First Edition: August 2003
ISBN 0-9710846-8-8

Library of Congress Cataloging-in-Publication Data

Fink, Jennifer.
Burn / Jennifer Natalya Fink.
p. cm.
ISBN 0-9710846-8-8
1. Utopian socialism—Fiction. 2. Middle aged women—Fiction. 3. Communal living—Fiction. 4. Jewish women—Fiction. 5. Mute persons—Fiction. 6. Socialists—Fiction. 7. Boys—Fiction. 8. Jews—Fiction. I. Title.
PS3606.I54B87 2003
813'.6—dc21

2003007811

Suspect Thoughts Press
2215-R Market Street, PMB #544
San Francisco, CA 94114-1612
www.suspectthoughts.com

Suspect Thoughts Press is a terrible infant hell-bent to publish challenging, provocative, stimulating, and dangerous books by contemporary authors and poets exploring social, political, queer, and sexual themes.

Acknowledgments

Thanks to Greg Wharton and Ian Philips: editors, visionaries, and comrades-in-arms.

Thanks to Frances Sorensen for her friendship, love, and terrific author photo.

Thanks also to my friends and fellow-travelers: D. Travers Scott, Valarie J. Moses, Matt Bernstein Sycamore, Michael Cunningham, Kate V. Hawes, Edward Albee, John Edward McGrath, Fred Leebron, Martin Hyatt, Frances Sorensen, Kiera Coffee, Sonya Leathers, Sikivu Hutchinson, Penelope Treat, Kelly Tzvia Washburn, Ellen Blum, Theresa M. Senft, Wendy Alker, Juliet Faithful, Michael Hyman, Jackie Frost, The Gorilla Press Girls, the late Heather Lewis and Lawrence Steger, my official and unofficial families, my students, and my parents, the Drs. Gerald and Rosalie Fink. My beloved grandparents, Adina and Hal Lewis, inspired me to fight the good fight. I am grateful to the Constance Saltonstall Foundation and the Edward F. Albee Foundation for providing me with artists' residencies. They gave me the time, support, and open sky to listen to Sylvia and Simon.

Portions of the novel *Burn* (Chapter 0-III) first appeared in *Texts and Textures*, the Constance Saltonstall Foundation's 2002 online chapbook (www.saltonstall.org).

For Jon Keith Brunelle

Love's the boy stood on the burning deck
trying to recite "The boy stood on
the burning deck." Love's the son
  stood stammering elocution
  while the poor ship in flames went down.

Love's the obstinate boy, the ship,
even the swimming sailors, who
would like a schoolroom platform, too,
  or an excuse to stay
  on deck. And love's the burning boy.

—Elizabeth Bishop, "Casabianca"

0.

They rest in your lap, they sit, they wait. So well-behaved. Tightly knit, like the closest of families.

Your hands. I still can't stop thinking about your fingers. I rehearse each one before I go to sleep, starting with the left pinkie, ending with the right. Oh, that final pinkie.

They sit, they rest, they clasp. This was one of the joys of having you in my house: you sit, creating a lap on which to clasp your hands together. Each finger laces around its doppelgänger, facing its twin. They clasp like, like nothing but your hands.

If you were here, I'd take out my sewing kit and mend. I'd thread my way through your fingers, twisting and tightening until they squeeze together, blushing scarlet down to the palms, a web of white lines forming where the thread cuts into the flesh. And then I'd sew the rest of you, arms into legs, press your flat stomach down to your thighs, weave you together into a basket. I wouldn't be the first to take you in pieces.

For you were made in pieces, one delicate limb at a time. Or perhaps on an assembly line, Taylorized, a dozen hands at once, a baker's dozen of legs per batch, an extra thrown in in case of defective workmanship. But even so, Simon, teams of craftsmen would still be needed to forge you, weld arm to torso, torso to leg. It could take months of work to design such a specimen.

Or perhaps not. Maybe you were a quickie, done in one long night in a sweatshop, strictly non-union, the machinery working late into the third shift. Those machines get hot. They spew out legs, thighs, hands, even fists, if they're not monitored properly. Just one spark, the foreman, an old guy named Little Eddy, warns the young guys on the line, and the whole fuckin' place blows. So you'd better, whaddayacallit, *be careful.*

Be careful. The first words you heard. Your ears were still molten when you heard them. Synapses, cilia, circuits: were they imprinted at that exact moment, shaped

around the sounds?
  Be careful.

I. Hands, Feet

So let's start with before. Feet first. Bare and white, his toes peeked out from beneath the shiny green leaves of my tomato plants. I glanced out at the garden to see if the soil needed watering, so I saw the feet first. I watched them for a few minutes, mesmerized by the carefully clipped toenails, before it occurred to me to look up and see whose feet they were.

It was a man. A naked man stood in my garden. A short naked man, sweating in the hot June sun. He faced my tomato plants like they were a wall, pissing away on them. I squinted, fingers fishing in my apron pocket for the glasses that would reveal who the hell was pissing in my garden. As the lenses sharpened the man into focus, I saw it was a boy.

Just a boy, on the edge of thirteen, maybe younger. Or older; a few straggly blond hairs roughened his chin. He shook his thing free of pee and scratched his chest and stood there, glaring. A kid. His eyes scanned my house, my garden. Something about his stance, the way he straightened his back and tilted his head to one side, gave me the odd sensation that he was listening for orders.

His feet were firmly rooted behind my Big Boy Burpees, the kind the catalogue advertises as featuring a big steak-tomato flavor, robust ruby color, and a bush habit. And indeed, even then, when they were still green, the tomatoes were meat-red inside, like raw steak. The feet were small and narrow, outdoor feet, yellow calluses visible on the sides.

I stood and watched the feet for a full minute or two. They didn't move. The Burpees swayed on the vine, the hot June wind nudging them back and forth. But the feet remained planted.

I didn't investigate. Not that time. I figured it could just be a Colony kid, playing hide-and-seek, waiting to be caught. But that didn't make sense. A regular kid would never stand so still.

I turned away from the window and went to turn the radio on, *no rain expected. At the tone, the time will be six forty-five* A.M. *Beep!* I flipped it off, distracted by the foreign body in my soil. Whose kid was it? With only seven families left, I knew all the Colony kids by face if not by name. Let's see: there's that Goldstein girl with the lisp. As I measured out the coffee, I ran down the list: Mady's Joseph with the drool on his sweater; Shep and Gladys' zaftig Lucy, the Feldsteins' brats, whaddya call them?...but they were all grown and gone already.

I looked back at the boy. His face was too pale, too raggedy to be a Colony kid's anyway. Maybe some poor relative from the City is visiting one of the families, I reasoned. The Goldsteins: they've got carloads full of cousins that come in from Brooklyn, Queens, Jersey. Or the Katz's cousins, maybe.

Or maybe not. I watched the boy pick a scab off the side of his leg, and then pick another one on the other leg, so symmetrical. He could just be a runaway, fresh off the train. He wakes and it's no longer the city outside. Trees lean into the road and the dark and the road. He feels not dirty, no, not cheap, either, despite the three fives folded up in his trousers pocket that the man in the gray suit had stuffed there after they left the hotel. He feels like James Dean: mean and clean, striding through a drive-in flick, one of those j.d. specials where everything's scrubbed and shiny, even the beatnik hangouts. Yeah, he's a real-live movie beatnik, daddyo! He laughs, wishing he had someone to share the joke with.

The train stops, pulling up at an unfamiliar crossroads. He sits up in his seat and gets off, not caring where the hell he is, anywhere but Lewisboro. He looks north, towards goddamn Lewisboro. If he were James Dean, he'd light a cigarette and push up the collar on his jacket, but instead he takes out his bandanna and slips it over his neck like a scarf or a noose or a pirate.

Is that how he came? Perhaps. I looked away, flipping the radio to 94.3 WQXR, my station, *At the tone it will be seven* A.M. *Stay tuned for News and Views. Beep!,* and when I glanced back, he was gone. I was glad; I didn't want to be worrying about tomato boys with bush habits messing up my garden.

But the next morning, there he was again, feet digging into the soft fertilized earth. He was peeing again, facing me this time, aiming a steady stream straight at my tomato plants. This time, I saw more than feet.

He really could be a spy. Were there more, planted behind each of the, what was it now, seventeen houses in the Colony? Most of the houses were already abandoned, but the planters might not know that. One fake kid per house?

An electronic buzzing noise was audible, even through the glass windows. I cocked my head: yes, it was coming from him. ZZZZZZZSssss. His mouth wasn't moving; his lips were shut tight, but that sound kept buzzing. A spy? A robot spy? I'd heard about the labs where ex-Nazis grew strange men the exact size and shape of boys.

I walked down our driveway, out onto Old Colony Road, and strode up to the Feinsteins' gray saltbox to see if there was a boy in their tomatoes, too. Their garden didn't look so good; the snap peas were overripe, wrinkling on the vine like old green men.

They've fled, I thought angrily. Those Feinsteins, they know about the spies, and they've gone back to their brownstone in Brooklyn. They'll let the bush beans, heirloom tomatoes, even the late-summer broccoli rot until the Feds are gone. Smart cookies, those Feinsteins. But the Feds are smarter. There'll be a small blond boy in their garden one day in Brooklyn, Queens, California, or wherever the hell they end up. They'll get them.

I walked back up the road to my driveway. Our garden was on the side of the house, out of view of the front, so I couldn't see if the boy was still there. I didn't want him to see me watching him. Bide your time, Sylvie, I told myself. Be careful.

So I walked as quietly as possible up the driveway

and back into my house, hoping he wouldn't hear my thighs rubbing together as I strode. My fat thighs make funny noises, like two old ladies sighing at a bridge game, and I don't like other people listening to them.

Once I was back inside my house, I made myself a cup of coffee: not the instant drek my Max preferred, but the real McCoy. I tried moving slowly, casually, no big deal, mister, just making my slow-drip coffee, in case he was watching me. Finally, I poured my coffee in a big gray mug, no cream, no sugar, set my chair in front of the kitchen window, and sat down, leaning back and crossing my legs. Only then did I let myself gaze out the window, as if I didn't care if there were a million blond boys pissing around in my tomato plants.

But he was gone. All that was left were four indentations near the tomato plants, where his feet had dug into the ground. High arches: each footprint made two marks, where the heel and toes pressed down, but nothing in the middle. Between the footprints, the earth was dark.

Pee is bad for tomato plants. It's awful for the soil—drains it of nutrients, murders the roots. It's too acidic for tomatoes; only pine trees need all that acid. And we don't have any pines in our yard. I stared out at the footprints, noticing the darkened splotch of earth beside them. Goddamn pisher, ruining my tomatoes.

Pulling out a pack of red licorice from my gardening pants, I ripped into the candy. "Goddamn little pisher!" I yelled between mouthfuls. Ridiculous!

The phone rang. I picked it up and heard a throat clear, a cough, and a click click. Then, only dead air.

I folded up the licorice wrapper carefully and put it in my pocketbook, as though nothing was wrong. Using a pencil from my purse as a toothpick, I cleaned my gums. I put the pencil back.

Now what?

I dialed Gladys, to see if she was having phone buggers, too.

"Hello?"

"Hi, Gladys."

"Sylvia." She said my name like it was a fact answering a question: what is the state capital of New Jersey? Trenton. What is the name of the woman with the reddest hair in Sylvan Lake? Sylvia. Gladys turned single words into pronouncements.

"Gladys. Is there anything funny with Nebraska?"

She laughed. We had our little code words; Sheppie had insisted on it since January. *Nebraska* for phone bugs, *Mickey Rooney* for meetings, *goldenrod* for danger.

"Nebraska. Oh, yesiree, Nebraska sure is acting up again. Full of ears, if you follow."

I followed. "Me too. Nebraska is making all kinds of odd sounds. Coughs, wheezes, and then, nothing. The old girl is just full of it."

"Well, you bring it up at the meeting — uh, Mickey Rooney. Don't forget: at two tomorrow, we're having a Mickey Rooney."

"Yeah, I'll be there. If Nebraska hasn't gotten me first."

"Sylvie. Darling. Oy, such a card. You take care and don't miss the meet— Mickey Rooney."

"Of course not, darling. Give my love to Shep."

So Gladys was having the bugs today, too. She was, I was, probably everyone was. It had started three weeks ago: random bugging, no pattern. But now it seemed like every other call a fishy sound filled the receiver. Between the phone bugs and the Mickey Rooneys, I forgot about the tomato pisser.

But the next day, there he was again. I caught him in the act, or finishing the act, at least: he was jiggling his thing, shaking off the last of the pee.

I squinted to get a closer look: uncircumcised. Not one of ours.

He noticed me watching and threw a glare back through the glass doors, but stood his ground. I froze, my cheeks burning. Nothing moved, except that gold trickle wending its way through the tomato plants. There was silence, no buzzing this time. I stared at him, and he stared back as he jiggled off the last drop.

Definitely a spy, I decided. Who else would stare me down in my own garden?

He started to pee again, holding his thing carefully, as though it might escape his grasp. Does this boy do anything but pee? His piss was bright yellow, like a neon gas sign, FILL UP HERE. How did they get it so yellow? Did he drink a special tea? Is his piss loaded with poisons, invisible to the eye? They must know that I eat my tomatoes raw off the vine, unwashed, with just a dash of salt.

My lips tensed into my tight old-lady smile. I watched, holding myself still in that smile, as he peed in my plants.

He peed in a thick stream, steady and even and juicy. I pictured raspberries, raspberries out of season, with that whiskery fuzz that covers them when they're not quite fresh. I'd squeeze the liquid out of them, straight on to my tongue. Watch those hairs!

*

Then it was later. And he was gone. And I was outside, gardening.

I don't know how I got there. All I remember is that I was in the kitchen and then I was in the garden.

*

As I came to, my thoughts raced. Did he have some special chemical in his pee that even at a distance, through air, walls, glass, could stun me as he made his escape? How did he get me out here? Did he slip me a, whaddyacallit, a mickey? What the hell was going on?

I shook my head, trying to clear my mind. Don't think crazy thoughts now, Sylvie old girl. There was no boy; it was just some ferkakte hot-flash dream. It was afternoon, late June and hot, and I was frozen. Maybe I'd come outside to garden, fallen asleep right in the middle, and now here I was.

My hands were numb inside my gardener's gloves from too much mulching. I'd been outside gardening for longer than I'd realized. Dead man's hands, I thought as I peeled the gloves off each gray finger.

I went inside and washed my hands under hot water in the sink until the life came back.

II. Fans

Louie was making accordion fans by folding up some old blue paper flyers about snow removal. He creased them unevenly, trying to get the job done too quick, handing out one while starting to fold another.

The six other raggedy remainders sat on wooden folding chairs in a circle with their blue fans. The Barn was hot and dank: like a real barn, full of seven sweaty animals. Some didn't even bother to make fanning gestures; they just held the fans still in their laps. Others, thinking this might be an important new document, unfolded their fans, read the notice about the change in our policy on snowplows, wrinkled their sweating brows in confusion, realized the notice was dated "February 1953," just some damn memo from last winter, and crumpled them up. But there was no garbage can, so they, too, had to hold the crushed paper in their laps.

We didn't sing. As I sat down, I wondered when it was exactly that we'd stopped opening meetings with a round of the "Internationale," then a workers' song like "Union Maid" or "Joe Hill," and finally "The Star-Spangled Banner": an odd troika I didn't miss.

"Comrades, Workers!" Shep bellowed. "Let's start. Agenda?" Always an agenda with Sheppie. He was a real commandante, my Shep, straight out of the ranks of ILGWU, the worst sort, the kind who actually enjoys meetings. I always hated that about him, even back when those gray blue eyes turned me wild.

The fanners kept fanning; the crumplers crumpled. I folded.

"Which of you momzers was supposed to make up the agenda?" Shep was neither a fanner, folder, or crumpler. He hadn't bothered to take a fan at all. Instead, Sheppie rubbed his beard. Party leaders always sport these bushy beards; even the ones like Shep, who lack much hair on top, managed the full comrade beard. Nobody spoke. He rubbed his beard again, and glared. I thought of the stray hairs on the boy's chin, like specks of dill scattered in a potato salad.

"Gladys? I think it was you." Shep talked to her like she was his inept secretary, not his wife. "Nu, Gladys?" he repeated. Everyone looked down at their fans, hoping it would be over fast.

Gladys snorted, pushing her glasses up her nose, fanning furiously. "No siree. It most certainly was *not* my job. For chrissakes, Sheppie, let's just get started already, agenda or no agenda. We all know what we need to discuss here, nu?" She scowled at Shep, and smiled at us.

Talk, talk, and more talk. *The thing here is...Nu you alter kockers! Don't you see that...But see here, you're forgetting what Bakunin wrote in...To hell with the lot of you! I say...Well I say...*

Talk about talk: *should we talk first or just go straight to it and vote? Should the Central Committee decide or should we all vote? Should we, should we not?*

Only seven of us left, and still it took hours to talk each item into the grave! I put my fan in my purse, thinking of Rose squirreling away dinner rolls at restaurants, only to forget to remove them when she gets home. We're all squirrelers in my family, but my sister is the worst. Rose and rolls: what a pair. My mother, she would take care to remember whatever she'd hidden in her purse, distributing the stale booty for days after our monthly outing to the diner on Avenue J: "Who wants rolls? Girls? Rolls? It's a shame to let them go to waste." Rose never remembers to distribute; it's the squirreling she prizes. She gives me a crooked grin each time she opens her purse and pops them in, as if she's pleased with herself for remembering to steal. Me, I never bother with rolls. Who needs all the crumbs? It's paper that finds its way into my purse: programs, notices, store receipts, scribbled grocery lists, quotes, notes, the odd newspaper article. Paper always finds me.

I played with my blue fan, half-listening, unfolding it carefully as Louie made a motion. "Everybody but the CCC gotta leave now." Elaine left the room, grinning like it was an honor to be the last follower. And then it was the six of us, the Central Committee of the Sylvan Lake Colony, or Colony Central Committee, CCC, such a big name for six people representing seven. Louie and Shep always insisted on giving fancy-shmancy names to everything. They'd have named each tree if they could: the Lenin Freedom Spruce, the Marx Manpower Maple.

The big talkers—Gladys, Shep, Joe, Mady—talked:

"We need to dissolve ourselves, fast, now. Today." Gladys wanted the quick fix, of course.

"No, no. That's exactly what the bastards want. We need to sit tight, and wait 'til this blows over. Then, the Revolution will sweep over the whole country and we'll be on the front lines of Justice." Mady was a heel-digger, a head-burier: the worse it looked for us, the harder she'd cling to the old Party line. Revolution Now! Revolution Forever! Revolution Today! Or next Wednesday.

"That's all talk." Joe narrowed his baggy eyes and rubbed his chest. "Comrades, there isn't gonna be a revolution; we gotta cover our asses before they fry us up and serve us to McCarthy with a side of potatoes. I ain't kidding, Sheppie." Joe Schwartz never was one to kid.

"What we need is strategy, a solid strategy. We need to get the whole Party leadership in on this, the boys from Brooklyn, the tool-and-dye crowd." Sheppie got the last word, of course.

Fans, coughs, loud dissension. The noise level rose. Joe sneezed, shpritzy and loud. He wiped his nose vigorously on his unfolded fan. Short and stocky, built like a wrestler with a street hood's brilliantined black crew cut, Joe was the youngest and toughest member. The other young guys were long gone, back to the city or off to the suburbs the second they'd smelled trouble, but not Joe. He'd worked the line, he'd fought the bastards in Spain, and he'd been in with the wise guys, the *real* wise guys down on Delancey. He'd broken a few necks and kicked a few asses along the way, and he wasn't about to let us forget about it. "Joltin' Joe," the boys kidded, though he never had DiMaggio's calm. Joe was always wiping or rubbing something: he rubbed his chest when he talked, in a harsh nervous motion over his heart. Elaine, his dopey wife, grimaced as he rubbed, but I never found it repulsive when Joe did these slightly disgusting things: it just seemed violently energetic, as though a little explosion was coming out of his nose or hand or tap-tapping foot.

"Face facts, folks." Joe was still rubbing as he talked. "They're closing in on us. They've got us but good: phones bugged, secret agents, even undercover spies." He glanced meaningfully at each person in the room. Could one of us be one of them? "We gotta think smart. Let's lay low, duck down until the capitalists eat their own goddamn tails. They're out for Commies, and they're gonna find themselves a Commie or two to fry if we let 'em."

Sheppie started humming the chorus of the "Internationale" defiantly. "Arise ye workers from your slumbers, arise ye prisoners of want." A few others joined in, off-key, half-hearted. Joe glowered at Shep. I fanned myself, not singing.

"Listen, Comrades! I got a plan. Otherwise, it's gonna be a goddamn inquisition here," Joe shouted over the dying "Internationale," rubbing himself with extra vigor. "We go private. Divvy up the property, the crops, the tools; hell, even our houses. On paper, at least, Sylvan Lake will be just another lousy Levittown."

Shouts, harrumphs, a few loud protests. I was getting dizzy from the heat, the smell of sweaty foreheads, all Joe's crazy ideas. We were going to change our papers? Turn capitalist? Through paper? I imagined the blue paper fans turned into crisp dollar bills, five clutched in each person's hand, fanning dollars like mad.

More shouts, arguments, griping. I couldn't pay attention. The boy's nails upon his knees, one leg, then the other, symmetrical, the twin twinge of relief and pain beneath the nail, eyes tearing as he scratches, iris veined gray like a sultan cabbage, left leg, right leg, harder, my legs tingling in sympathy. And then it was over.

"Enough discussion," said Joe. "We've been going

back and forth for weeks. It's dopey; we all know what the score is. Comrades, workers: it's over. *The Colony is over.*" He paused, as if someone were going to challenge him. But nobody did; he'd said the one and only thing that could put a lid on this gang. I stopped rubbing my knees. "Okay. So that's settled. Now we need a plan, a real plan. I say we need to turn the Sylvan Lake Collective Colony into private property, and fast. We gotta wipe out every last pinko aroma before the Feds set in."

Before the Feds set in...or are they already in? Here, right here, who knows who has turned, who is taping, who is talking, who will get on the 8:10 Local right after this meeting and head back into the city, stop for a quick beer in Grand Central, then talk fast and cheap to who knows who in god knows which office?

Nobody said this. But eyes weren't met, Shep turned away, and everyone wondered who else was listening.

"So, Sheppie, Joe, what about the Barn?" Gladys piped in, saving us from the Feds. She was always good with the details, that Gladys. She was a big gun back in the Doll and Toy Maker's Union, moving from factory piecework to organizing the whole shop in no time flat. Gladys the Detail Gal. Gladys, Sheppie's Gal. Or so she liked to think.

"The Barn?" Louie didn't get it.

"Yeah, the Barn," I echoed. "Who's gonna own the Barn, if everything's gonna be private property, nu?" My own words surprised me. I'd never really liked the Barn. I hate fakes, and the Barn was Queen of the Phonies.

Now, I knew barns. I'd lived right beside one, on my cousin's New Jersey dairy farm. I'd lived out there for a year when I was eight, when my mother couldn't feed all six of us and figured that, out on a farm, at least there'd be food. And there was: sluggish cows, surly ducks, chickens, chicken shit, hens, cats, and too many cousins clamoring for more. Our barn meant food, work, shit, shelter. We never gave the Jersey barn a second thought: it was the animals who worried us, the sick or pregnant or not-pregnant or dying animals.

But this Barn was no barn. It was a fake, from the wood beams, chemically treated to look dark and weatherworn, to the big barn doors, found at auction in Queens, to the smell of straw, remnants of a failed attempt at making a hayride for the kids one year on May Day. The straw, bought from a local farmer for fifty cents a bale—an outrageous price!—still scented the air with a dry, furry musk that reminded me of all the horses who had never set hoof in our barn.

And now here we were, waxing sentimental about a barn that had never held a single animal, save the occasional field mouse. Yet I hated the thought of somebody owning it. We built it together: Max, me, Shep, and a few of the others in the room. It was ours—vermin, wooden beams, overpriced hay, spies and bugs and all. It seemed strange, embarrassing, even, to discuss the Barn's fate while sitting within its walls. I glared at Joe, hating him for betraying the Barn, filled with passion for the Barn, our drekky Barn, our own true fake. I had never really thought much about the Barn before, but now that I did, I confess: I was in love with the Barn.

"Who's gonna get the Barn?" I repeated.

Nobody answered. Louie furrowed his brows. Before he went bald, he was handsome, in a hairy short-guy sort of way. He knew hardware, he could fix a sink, he could build a road. A real mensch, a fixer, a straight shooter, a loyal comrade who didn't need to debate Lenin versus Trotsky to find the right side of the fence. But now, egg-bald, with such bushy gray eyebrows, he looked like a kook. Looking at him, I thought how the Feds would love to get a guy like this, a literal egghead, with movie-monster mad-scientist eyebrows and a crazy grin to boot. They wouldn't care what a regular guy he was; one look at that mug, and off to the Chair he'd go. His egghead brows furrowed a moment longer, and then finally he spoke. "Well, I guess we could, I don't know, turn it into a town hall or something.

Whaddya think?"

The room exploded in dissension: *whaddya mean, turn it into a town hall, we should tear it down, we should dig in our heels and stay, we should we should...*

Louie just shook his head as the volume got louder. Nobody was listening to him anymore.

Everyone talked at once. Mady Feld shouted at Shep, "In Utah the Trotskyites turned their main building into a revolutionary fortress. A real fortress, I tell you!" While Shep announced to the general public, "A few hundred bricks I need, and I'll build a wall around the whole damn Colony that the Feds can't stick their schmucks through!"

Gladys grabbed my hand and quietly but energetically began whispering to me about her plan for building an in-ground pool behind her house, "where my azaleas are now. Once this fracas is over, and the rest of you leave, I'll be building my pool, and you—"

This was too much. I turned to Louie, cutting her off. "A town hall, eh Louie?" I'd rather hear about Louie's latest pipe dreams than about Gladys' pool plan.

"A town hall, I tell you," Louie boomed.

Of course it was Sheppie who got the floor back. "Town hall? You're talking the crazy talk, Louie. Next thing, you'll be suggesting we join the I-Like-Ike gonifs," Sheppie scoffed.

Everyone laughed. I think it was the phrase "town hall" that did poor Louie in that day. Nobody knew from town halls; we were Brooklyn kids, spawned from stoop ball mated with sweatshops on hot nights down on Avenue J.

I thought of the boy. Naked, outside a white colonial town hall, in stocks like those heavy wood contraptions the Puritans used, pissing on himself. The dark wood glistened like aluminum foil in the sunlight, brighter than metal. Nothing moved but the piss dribbling down his thigh.

The conversation was getting louder, rowdier. Joe and Louie were standing too close, shouting insults in each other's sweaty orange faces. *Goddamn Bakuninist! Trotskyite!*

Turncoat! Class Traitor!

Too loud, too hot. The boy in stocks stayed in my head, drowning out the Barn.

Of course I didn't mention the boy in my garden. Instead, I got up, pushed my folding chair away, clutched my paper fan, and walked straight out of the Barn into my bed.

On top of the unmade covers, lying back in our four-poster, I fanned myself. How lovely it would be to have a room as blue as the blue paper fan. The white walls, green carpet, green covers inherited from Rose: they would all be so much more elegant in an eggshell blue.

The stocks slowly faded as I thought of my room turning blue, the Barn, too: everything repainted. I could see the boy and stocks blue, too, but I concentrated hard on my room, instead: the heavy ceiling fan grumbling as it turned, the covers bunched at my feet, and the walls, too white, ready for blue.

III. Spies, Tomatoes

The next day, I spied him again. I was up early, ready to garden, but it was overcast, the sky clouding up like a gloomy girl on the verge of tears, so I decided to stay inside and paint my bedroom blue.

By noon I was tired, and sick to death of the smell of turpentine. I put the paint cans, tarp, turpentine, and brushes back in the garage, showered the blue spots off my skin, and went into my kitchen to drink some coffee and wait for the paint to dry.

He wasn't peeing this time. No, he was eating a green tomato, biting into the tough skin. I watched him chew, the sour juice dribbling down his chin, his teeth so big and healthy, with a little chip on the front lefty. I could picture his baby teeth, straight white squares, smaller than these. He bit twice and chewed. Were they stored in a gray velvet box somewhere, stashed away in a drawer in his mother's vanity? After gobbling down the tomato, he pulled another off the vine and started in on it, naked and chewing. Bite, bite, chew: a waltz.

Maybe he's just a hungry boy, I thought as I swallowed down my coffee and hunted for some licorice in the pantry. A local kid, one of those Lewisboro boys you see riding on the back of their Pa's trucks. Maybe he'd had too much hooch with his buddies last night, and they'd stripped him naked and dumped him in my garden, yukking it up as they drove off in their beater. Or maybe they've finally come for me.

In a way, it would be a relief. I'd been waiting for them. Waiting for the phone to ring, for an official, too-friendly voice asking if you happen to know anyone—not you yourself, of course, Mrs. Edelman, but perhaps one of your neighbors, the Goldsteins, the Schwartzs, or that crazy old widow Mrs. Mady Feld née Horowitz—who is a member or friend of the Communist Party? We'd all been waiting for that call, preparing a response that we wouldn't mind hearing played back on one of those giant reels of shiny brown tape. Oh no, I don't know anyone or anything at all. I'm not the sort of gal who mixes much with politics. And I don't really know my neighbors. I spend most of my time in my garden, you see.

Or maybe they're smoother than that, adding the personal touch: Mrs. Edelman? Mrs. Sylvia Edelman? Jim Kantrowitz here. We went to P.S. 281 together. Remember me, Skinny Jimmy? Well, I'm not so skinny anymore, heh heh, but I'm still a crack chemistry whiz. How's Mr. E.? Oh. So sorry to hear that. He was one swell guy, your Max was. Well, I don't mean to be a pest, but I thought you might still be in touch with some of the old gang, say, Mady Feld, or Sheppie, uh, Shep and Gladys Goldstein? I'm trying to track them down for some official nonsense—yeah, I'm with the Bureau now—and I thought you might have a clue as to where in hell they all are now. Sheppie, what a gonif he was, huh? Such chutzpah, that one. Those were the good days, right Sylvie?

And without thinking I'd be telling him all about Gladys, Sheppie, Mady, maybe even mention a few he didn't think of. That's how they get you. One minute it's reminiscing about the yearbook, then it's the fellow-travelers list, and before you know it your ass is sizzling away on the Big Chair like a fatty slice of bacon. Better to forget about the good old gang, before the wrong ones remember you. Better to forget about Mady, Sheppie, even Charlie, who's dead what, twenty years by now?

I thought of Sheppie as I brooded about all this and watched the boy. They had similar cheekbones: high and wide, then curving in suddenly toward the chin. Cast from the same mold, as my father would say.

But I wasn't interested in molds, not me. My heart belongs to templates. I learned all about them from Max, back when he had the print shop. Templates remind me of those Greek gods we read about back in Mrs. Cohen's class: marble-limbed, impersonal vessels swooping down from on high to bother the foolish mortals below, shaping their destinies, yet remaining apart even as they grasp and fix whatever comes their way. I still appreciate a good template, a structure that stays still no matter how much garbage it's fed. What template did they use to get such fine cheekbones? What do the others look like, his manufactured "brothers" (or sisters? could there be girls, too? I can't imagine a girl-Simon; no, the facial hair gets in the way of that pretty picture)? This one could be a god, I decided, though certainly he's no Greek. He arched his eyebrows, meeting my gaze. High and blond, the brows gave his plain, even features a touch, just a light touch, of feminine glamour.

The clock in the hall struck twelve. Let him eat your tomatoes 'til he's sick, Max's dead voice piped in as the hammer-and-sickle clock began its routine. Forget about it, and he'll disappear in a few days. Spy or no spy, he'll be gone in a day or two if you just ignore him. I looked away and looked back. Such a face on this one!

The clock finished and Max faded. Time for another meeting at the Barn. Another round of mishegas and gibberish, everyone wanting to be top dog, captain of the ship even as it sinks.

I lingered a moment longer, my gaze dropping from the boy's brow to his lashes. I didn't notice the eyes, that time; just the lashes. They're too long for a boy, I thought as I bustled around the house to get ready. Too long for a girl, for that matter. A china doll's lashes, glued on one at a time. Doll face, you've got the cutest little doll face, I hummed as I left the house, not looking back at the boy.

IV. Entrances, Exits

I was late. Really late, too late for my entrance to even matter. Shep had the floor, and everyone else was sitting tight around the table, necks craning to catch each word, spellbound. He nodded in my general direction, but didn't stop talking as I strode into the Barn.

The air was charged, bristling with the effects of...what?

Sheppie's eyes were glistening. "So we don't do nothing until we hear from those alter kocker lawyers." Lawyers? "Then, we wrap everything up here, nice and clean. That's the only way." Sheppie leaned on his good leg, gesturing with big sweeping movements, waving his arm, head, and bad leg, like he was speaking to the ILGWA instead of a half-empty room of old Colony fonfers.

I looked around as I took a seat beside Gladys. No Louie; where the hell was he? Gladys was nodding along to Sheppie's voice, eyes lit up with adulation. Yes, Shep, oh yes, Sheppie boy, uh huh, yes, that's right, yes, yes. A hundred yeses in every nod.

Joe stood up, facing Shep, both hands moving along his chest. "But what about the resolution? We had a resolution here, Sheppie; we voted, it passed, the Colony was dissolved, end of story."

They had dissolved the Colony without me? I pulled out one licorice stick and then another, eating the second before I'd swallowed the first.

Joe kept it up. "And now you sail in here and tell me we're gonna wait while the Feds nail our asses while some goddamned fur-lined lawyer of yours futzes around?"

Sheppie smiled, patting his own beard gently like a lover's cheek. "Okay: so we dissolve the Colony. Fine. But that's not the end of it. Come tomorrow, some schlemiel has a little chat with Mr. Informer. Next thing you know, we'll be up to our ears in Feds; once they get one of us, once one member, *just one lousy member* turns coat, and the whole place will be crawling. They've been waiting for us to dissolve; it'll show the bastards that we've got something to hide." He turned towards the rest of us. "Don't you get it? The whole idea of dissolving the Colony stinks. It's a trap," he said evenly, not raising his voice, but looking straight at Joe.

"And you, Sheppie, you got an alternative?" Mady asked, squinting.

"I say, we talk to the lawyers and see if there's a way out of this. Maybe we incorporate, turn the Colony into a village. Those who want to stay, stay. Those who want to leave, leave. Either way, we're clean." Sheppie grinned, but nobody else was smiling. That smile—pressed against my cheek as we danced in the Barn on a Friday-night Colony dance when Gladys had gone to see her mother; Sheppie's hair combed back and fluffed up, leading me in a fox-trot, waltz, karubichka; my Evening of Paris in his nose, all the women with flowers in their hair, a rose for Rose, a violet for me—that smile nuzzling my ear, told nothing.

Joe wasn't smiling. "Wait a minute here. Comrades, as I understand it, Sheppie is proposing that we let the lawyers dissolve us. But we got our own laws here, based on justice, not a bunch of jackass lawyers. Am I right? We voted fair and square on the dissolution—"

Shep broke in. "A vote at which, I might add, neither myself nor Sylvia was in attendance!" I blanched at the mention of my name, coupled with Sheppie's. There were snickers.

"You want to do it all over again? Fine, Sheppie. Let's vote again, just for old time's sake." Good for you, Joltin' Joe. "Comrades, Workers! Resolved: the Sylvan Lake Collective is hereby dissolved. Each house will revert to private ownership. Gary Berg out in Forest Hills will handle the legal work. All who are with us, raise your right fist." Joe stared solemnly at us, his dark eyes piercing a hole through any challenge coming their way.

Everyone except Shep and Gladys raised their fists. Four to two: the fists had it.

"Comrades, Workers! Resolved: this is the

Collective Will of all Colony Comrades." Joe smiled, a gracious winner. Everyone was smiling back at Joe, like we'd voted for new picnic tables, or announced that somebody's cousin's niece was getting married. Mazel tov!

Shep shifted tactics. "Can I make a motion here, Joe? Nobody has to do nothing, now that we're dissolved, but I think we should get a second opinion on the legal mishegas. I mean, who is this 'Gary Berg' anyway? Is he a Party man? Does he know from colonies? How do we know he's not a fink? I got this guy Barry, you see, who's my cousin Al's brother. Barry Rogashevsky. He's a Comrade, a landsman."

"Yeah, a second opinion!" Gladys Sheppie-echoed.

Mady had to get her two or three cents in. "I know a lawyer. The Richters' son, Sammie, I think it was. You remember the Richters?"

"Sure, sure. Nice kid. And remember the Kantrowitzs? Their son Bobby's a lawyer now. Remember those skits he'd do about the ice cream man?"

And on it went. *Do you remember the Lebowitz boy? Good-looking kid, yeah. He's a lawyer now. Remember that summer he almost drowned his uncle in Lake Sylvan? And now he's a big macher in the city, just like his father!* Everyone and their monkey's uncle knew a good lawyer. I thought of the boy and his bones, cheek collar hip pointing out of his skin, ready to take flight, hands pressing against bone as he scratched a scab, my hand on his, my hand freed of flesh, all bone, oh to touch bone to bone. My fingers gripped the packet of licorice, sweating into its slimy skin.

The last word, always Sheppie stole it. "My pal Barry'll be in tomorrow at nine sharp to help us with the legal mishegas, so don't oversleep. And watch your phones, folks. Nebraska! Don't say nothing you wouldn't want to hear repeated in front of the stinkers from HUAC. See you tomorrow, Comrades. Good meeting, Joe." He winked at Joe, and then at me. "Oh—and Gladys and I got strawberries in from the patch. They came up really good this year. So come by before ten tonight if you want some strawberries and sour cream."

Strawberries and stinkers from HUAC: I couldn't keep from blending them together in my mind. Strawberries do have a stink to them, if they get too ripe. Like cheap wine, vinegary and rancid. And HUAC chases reds, strawberry reds. I imagined a man in a dark gray suit chasing after a giant strawberry with a butterfly-catching net. The Colony had dissolved, and nobody had told me? Or had it really, since we had to vote about it all over again? I was sweaty, my palm and armpits swampy. The beginnings of a hot flash, or just the heat? HUAC and strawberries and Shep's sour-cream lawyers...it was too hot for all this; I could have used another of Louie's blue fans.

Despite the fact that Sheppie had officially ended the meeting, everyone was still yakking away. *What should we do? Should we even trust this Gary bastard? Or should we listen to Sheppie, and let this Barry Bigwig handle it? But what if Sheppie's already in the Feds' pockets? What if they move in tomorrow, lock us all up? Isn't there still a way to save the Colony, go underground, go somewhere they can't catch us, go to Moscow, go anywhere? Or should we hold our ground? Whaddya think?* Round and round the talk went in crazy eights, always ending where it had started. *What should we do?*

I was getting dizzy from too much talk going nowhere. Spies, strawberries, lawyers. And the boy.

"So Sylvie, you made plans to leave, or are you sticking it out until the bloody end?" Joe asked me, frowning.

I gave an ambiguous shrug. "I don't know. This heat, it's just too much for me." He nodded, looking grave, not sure what to say.

I really couldn't bear another minute of it. So I nodded to everyone and walked out. What did I need them for? Traitors, no-goodniks, Trotskyites, turncoats every last one of them.

Max's bluster buoyed me as I reached the door and looked back at the room, at Shep, Mady, and Gladys, all yap-yapping away, ignoring me. My skin was clammy, my clothes clinging like a wet bathing suit. Not a true comrade in the whole lot. To hell with them. To hell with their strawberries.

"'Night, Bunny. You behave," Shep winked at me as I walked out the door. But he didn't follow.

Back home, I pouted in my kitchen. Nobody even cared that I'd left. Here I was, alone in my kitchen, while everyone else was debating the end of the goddamn world. The end of the Colony. *My* Colony. I pulled out all the bells and whistles: my bottom lip curled out, my cheeks reddened with rage, and small tears gathered in the outer corners of my eyes. Sulky Sylvie, Max would've teased. But with no audience, the pout lost its moxie pretty fast. The tears dried, and my cheeks cooled down, and the lip resumed its normal station on my face. Nobody called, "Hey, what's the trouble, Red?", or any of the other foolish things the folks on Avenue J would've yelled.

I heard the rustle of leaves. Fallen leaves? In June? I must be going meshugge already! Drowsily, I realized that the rustling was coming from inside my own house. Mice? Rats? Or, worse, raccoons? Spies didn't occur to me. I was too tired for spies.

It was coming from right in front of me. The pantry! I grabbed a mop and made my way over to our walk-in pantry, hoping nothing would walk out. If Max could see me now! Hardly your scaredy-Sylvie-cat, eh, Maxie?

I opened the pantry door slowly with one hand, lifting the mop so that I could strike the bugger but good. I'd known plenty of rats in my time. But this could be worse: a raccoon. Or a nest of raccoons. Or—

"Christ!"

He darted out, making a run for the kitchen door, but it was locked shut. I always locked it at night, with a Yale lock, the kind they make special for sliding-glass doors, that Max installed the year we had the burglary at the Barn. Cornered, he smiled a big sloppy grin at me. And darted back into the pantry.

It was the same boy. The tomato boy. Still naked, but with a red farmer's bandanna tied over his head and a red-plaid satchel beside him. A poised pirate. Bare-assed. No buzzing this time; just the giggle. A scabby-kneed naked pirate, washed up onto my kitchen floor.

I ran after him, opening the pantry door again. He was curled up in a ball on his side, like a newborn hoping to crawl back in, surrounded by a bed of cleaning fluids. No such luck. He looked straight into my eyes and broke out into another giggle.

I'd had enough. If he hadn't giggled again, maybe I'd just have yelled at him, chased him out of my house, and that would have been the end of it. But that laugh tipped the scales right over. So I grabbed his neck and didn't let go.

But he grabbed, too. "Ow!" It was a shock to feel my nipple again. Not to feel pain, but my nipple, waving up. Pinkies, Max had called them.

The boy grabbed through the cloth of my dress, a light yellow cotton number. Ow, ow, ow. My mouth fell into his, right there among the old rags and mousetraps. His tongue was cold. My fingers were stuck on his face, pressing his skin, skull, sweat. A cold sweat perfumed with dirt and lemons.

Lemons? There are no lemon trees in my garden, I thought dizzily as I stroked his wet face, licking his neck, kissing his Adam's apple as it jumped up and down. Yet this acrid citrus flavor, I knew it, I'd tasted these lemons before, where, when, on whose skin?

His fingers stayed on my nipples, just nipples, touching them without touching the breast, only nipples, running hard to greet his greedy hands. And fingers, such fingers! The nails trimmed and filed, the tips uncalloused and pink, the fingers militant on my poor pinched nipples.

Love, love, love, I thought stupidly, panting. The lemon scent grew sourer. Perhaps this is part of their plan. They've doped up the Windex with some lemon-flavored love serum, only a drop or two necessary, the yellow carefully camouflaged by the Windex blue, just a few golden drops, not enough to turn it green, shake it all up, and then

BANG!

*

I don't remember who was where, who did what, or how long it all lasted. The mechanics don't stay. Only sweat, lemons, a cold tongue, and the dog tag.

I pressed his lips to mine, his tongue pushing mine open, my hand pulling off the scab, his tongue deliciously cold, a frozen snake. My mouth traveled his face, giddily kissing my way down until I hit bone.

Bone? No. Too cold to be bone. Metal.

A necklace? On a boy?

I opened my eyes. No, not a necklace: a metal chain, with a metal tag hanging from it. I fingered it like it was another sex organ, stroking it hard inside my mouth. I felt the surface grow uneven under my tongue. Was the metal dissolving? Was this a trick? It tasted bitter, metallic. Cyanide? Mercury? I gagged, pulling it out. I pulled the boy and the chain and its tag onto my lap to examine. He closed his eyes, feigning sleep.

No, the tag was not dissolving in my mouth; I was only tasting the inscription. S-I-M-O-N, it said, in girlish curlycued cursive etched into the metal. A name tag, dog tag, necklace.

"Simon?" His eyeballs flickered under his closed lids. I kissed his head in my lap. No response. I dropped Simon's tag. I wanted more. Running my hand the length of him, I tried to find some clue, a sign. But all I felt was a boy, his skin. A body. A scab. Where did he get so many scabs? They were too big to be mosquito bites. I touched the scab below the left knee carefully, not hurting it. It was an old one, hardened, bluish.

My nipples hurt. I moved his head off my lap and spooned myself around him.

"Simon says, Simon says," I chanted into his ear, nuzzling his face with my nose, twisting his bandanna playfully around his neck. He fluttered his doll lashes.

"Simon says, Simon says."

*

When I awoke, I was still sprawled in the bottom of the pantry. My legs hung out of the cupboard doors, two escaped convicts on the lam.

He was gone.

It was an evil dream, I decided, caused by one of those golems, miscarried babies who turn into cruel roaming angels, stirring up trouble in our sleep. Yes, the boy was at least half-golem.

Simon. What an unlikely name for a young boy. I said it out loud, feeling its shape in my mouth. "Simon."

*

I pulled myself out of the pantry, remembering all the gory details, lemons and dog tags, a nutso dream. That's what happens when you don't have a man, Sylvie, Max would've smirked. You just make one up in those dirty dreams of yours.

But what about this? The pink skin was puckered and chafed from too much mouth. I stood, naked, examining each nipple. Yes, there was no denying it: nipples had been sucked.

And there was other evidence. The bandanna was tied gaily around a bottle of pine-scented floor wax Rose had lent me. Beside it was the plaid satchel. I still smelled a hint of lemon.

I should have been horrified, I know. Shocked! What had I done? Outraged! What was that kid doing in my house, anyway? Ashamed! An old yenta like me, playing hanky-panky with some young hoodlum, and in my pantry, no less?

I opened up the satchel. There was nothing inside. It was a nice satchel, good plaid wool on the outside, black silk lining the inside. A rich man might give this satchel to his son on the first day of school. I closed it carefully, tears welling up in my tired eyes. I miss you, my darling Simon. I kissed the bandanna, oh so gently, and put it in the satchel.

My little pirate, I thought as I closed the satchel. My Simon, he's left me and run off to sea.

V. How He Came, How We Came

Did he come by railroad? Or did he set forth on foot from the basement office of a silent secret agency, marching alongside the highway, walking all the way up from Fifty-Seventh Street to Old Colony Road? How do they breed grown men to be so short? So convincingly boyish? Were his parents circus midgets, dolled up like children well into their forties? Was he specially trained to mimic the habits and gestures of children? Or did he just cling to his original boyhood antics, never needing to add or subtract a single gesture as the years passed?

Questions, too many questions. I crouched back into the pantry, the satchel on my lap, worrying. My head buzzed with goddamned questions as I knocked over the Windex bottle and cursed aloud. "Christ!" My neck ached from sleeping curled under there. I pulled myself out of the pantry and into the morning.

The kitchen was flooded with light, the bone glare of a cloudy day. A whole night, sleeping in the pantry! I walked to the kitchen table, my legs wobbly from lying folded up under the pantry for so long, and looked out the sliding-glass doors into the garden.

Simon's toes greeted me. He was sprawled on his back, asleep in the zucchini patch, the bottoms of his feet facing me. Dirty feet. Even from the kitchen, I could see streaks of dirt traveling up his feet all the way to his muscular thighs, swirled like the silt left on the highways after a storm. How did he get here? Did he come by bus? If I sniffed the arches, would I smell bus?

We came in buses. Thinking of the boy trekking out here by bus made me nostalgic. Those endless bus rides. Back in, what was it, '33, '34? They bussed us in on Friday evenings in those old clunkers borrowed from the Union. They were small, fitting only fifteen plus a driver, but on a good weekend we could fill a half-dozen of them. On Thursdays, the announcement would appear on the bulletin board by the lunch room: "Sylvan Lake—A Cooperative

Camp for Workers. Gather Strength for the Looming Fight! Good Food. Comradely Atmosphere. Proletarian Sports, Recreation, and Culture. Register at once! Bus Leaves 1800 7th Avenue, Corner 110th St. Every Fri. 6:30 P.M." I liked the idea of gathering strength for a looming fight: it reminded me of Popeye, chomping down a dozen cans of spinach. I could see the Fight himself, a big hairy man with the words "FIGHT" emblazoned on his chest, creeping up on poor Popeye as he opened and swallowed down can after can, his muscles finally popping up in the nick of time.

It was cheaper to sign up for the whole summer, but I only went for the weekend that first time. Gladys and Bella talked me into it. "Come on, what have you got to lose?" Bella cajoled. "Who knows, you might even have a good time for once!"

The trip was a caravan of bawdy Party songs and salami sandwiches. The buses stopped by the Lake, which I was disappointed to see was more like a large green pond—silvery-green, like the name would suggest—but they did have a real sand beach to accompany it. Back then, Sylvan Lake was only a summer colony. There were no real houses; only a dozen slipshod bungalows scattered beside the Lake on the corner of Old Colony Road and Danger Road. The Barn, the Lake: the Colony boys favored literal, impersonal names. Call a spade a spade, a colony road Colony Road, a twisting dead-end lane Danger Road. There was no room for fancy words at Sylvan Lake. "The Class Struggle, the only truth, needs no ornamentation," Sheppie would intone on those trips out to Sylvan Lake. He still had something of the yeshiva bucher about him then, always quoting the Great Sages of the Struggle, eyes buried in obscure party literature. "Buchers make the best bündists," as Bella told me once within Sheppie's earshot.

*

But I'm getting sidetracked. I was telling you about how we arrived at the Colony:

Sweaty from the bus ride, eager for proletarian sports, recreation, comrades and culture, we'd stream off the bus into the Barn like a bunch of Coney Islanders racing to the Wonder Wheel. We'd gather in the Barn for more folk songs, more salami sandwiches, and the all-important room assignments. Families got bungalows; everyone else was stuck with tents. Us single gals were stuck together, six to a rickety tent. Everyone shared one outhouse, a two-seater doused in chloride of lime that burned you but good if you weren't careful. "Watch your ass!" we'd yell whenever someone walked toward it, exploding in cackles no matter how many times we made the joke.

We'd pitch our tents on that carefully imported sand beach by the Lake, singing the "Internationale" as we worked:

Arise ye workers from your slumbers
Arise ye prisoners of want
For reason in revolt now thunders
And at last ends the age of cant.
Away with all your superstitions
Servile masses arise, arise
We'll change henceforth the old tradition
And spurn the dust to win the prize.

I always imagined the prize as I sang, a golden medal pinned to each worker's chest.

The "Internationale," sung off-key by everybody, everyday, punctuated every moment of life in the Colony. I would hear it as I fell asleep in my tent, between the uneven snores of the congested Queens girl sleeping beside me, long after the actual singing had ended. And then again in the morning, when our wake-up horn blasted it out:

So comrades, come rally
And the last fight let us face
The Internationale unites the human race.
So comrades, come rally

And the last fight let us face
The Internationale unites the human race.

They always made us sing the refrain twice, *So comrades, come rally....* It annoyed me, singing it the second time around. I'm facing the fight, I've joined, I'm getting goddamned mosquito bites all up and down my arms in a leaky tent for the Struggle. What more do you want from me? I'm here, I've joined, I'm fighting. I've come.

It was Bella who made us go. Lovely Bella, with her blond curls and Betty Boop laugh. She had just met a young man from one of the big fur outfits on 32nd Street. I forget his name, but he always had a gray wool cap on, even in the summer. Wool Cap was a fervent Leninite, an International Fur Workers organizer, a Worker's Club man, a hard-liner since his break with the Bakuninites. "You girls," he said one night as he walked us from our needle shop to the subway, treating us both to ices on the way, "you girls need to get out of the city." So Bella followed him and we followed Bella, all the way out to the Colony. Strange she was the first to turn. But being first was always second nature to Bella. When we got off the bus and ran down to the Lake that first day I came, Bella poured water down the front of her suit and exclaimed, "Ach a machia," oh what a pleasure, and everyone else did the same for the rest of that summer.

And where are Bella, Wool Cap, all the rest of the original fonfers now? I don't remember where I heard it, but the word on Wool Cap was that he'd been one of the first to fink. *Wool Cap, he's a known informant! a turncoat! a class traitor, that sonofabitch,* someone heard from someone's cousin's brother-in-law. And I believe it. The most truly devoted, the wild-eyed ones who spontaneously quote whole passages of *Das Kapital* at seder dinner, those are the ones who are the first to turn. Wool Cap. What an irritating schmuck he was. And now he's probably safe and sound in Levittown, Scarsdale, Edison Park, with Bella and Rose and the rest. Soon to be followed by Sheppie and Gladys and the rest of the rest. Oh, sure, I can see it now: Shep the Trotskyite, driving a green station wagon with wooden panels, first on his block to get the special rack-and-pinion steering; Shep the Righteous rigging the barbecue in the backyard so it can slow-broil a whole chicken; Shep and Gladys, hosting Tupperware on Sunday nights at the local synagogue. Maybe Wool Cap and his fat wife will join them for a game of canasta!

I grunted with satisfaction at the image of the comrades from Avenue J reunited at a temple barbecue. Sellouts, traitors, class enemies, turncoats, the whole lot of them just a bunch of bourgeois finks. Damn them all to capitalist hell! Damn Sheppie, extra. Double jinx on him, as Rose used to say.

Triple jinx. In a frenzy, I fixed a cup of coffee, jinxing and hexing Shep, Gladys, Bella, and even old Wool Cap, one at a time, forgetting all about the boy in my garden. Jinx them all to goddamn bourgeois hell. Jinx on you too, Max, wherever you are.

As I stirred the coffee, the jinxes subsided. I sipped and, eyeing the brown fluid, remembered the dirty brown feet outside. I put my glasses on, but didn't look out the window right away. Relax. Don't look too eager; it's unbecoming on a girl, Max would always say.

Gazing out into the garden, I caught sight of them. The left pinkie wiggled off an ant. Oh Simon, who built you such perfect toes? Each one its own piglet, each one evenly separated from the rest. Handmade, perfectly plumped, crafted one at a time. Imported. An old man with a messy beard works with a chisel and a magnifying glass, putting in a week's work of overtime on the third shift to finish your toes.

"I love your toes," I said out loud, surprised at how grave my voice sounded.

My finger reached for my nipple, still raw from the pantry. I closed my eyes, keeping the image of his perfect dirty feet in my head. This little piggy goes to market, but this one stays home with Sylvie. I'll pull off your big toe, pop it in my front pocket, and keep it. It will come off gracefully, a grape tugged and eaten off the vine in one gesture.

But there was no time for that. I had to go. To meet. Goddamn meetings. The meeting room in the Barn, filled with yammering voices, replaced the boy's feet in my mind's eye.

We're meeting to, to what? Write up the deeds? I opened my eyes, stopped with the nipple business, and looked back out in the garden. Talk to the lawyers? I tried to remember as I watched the boy get up, yawn, and play distractedly in the dirt, digging into the ground with a long branch. He slumped, stooping over like an old man who'd been on his feet too long. From here, I couldn't see his scabs. A lawyer, yes, that's right, Larry somebody, or was it Barry? Sheppie's lawyer boychik, he's coming to straighten things out, divvy up the spoils. I stuck out my tongue, thinking of all those pious conversations, back in the '40s when we winterized, about community property, collective ownership, the almighty Collective Will.

Goddamn hypocrites. I smiled, looking forward to the end of it all. I was sick of these endless meetings, secret agents, Party nonsense, money worries. This house will be mine, all mine at last, no longer Max's, and no longer a cell in the sick body of the Collective. I fingered my dress, thinking of the boy's scab, the rough feel of it.

Because really, there was no Collective anymore. Who were we kidding? We all had private bank accounts now, individual split-level houses, jobs in the city (and not as workers anymore, mind you; the men were all managers now, or owners of small shops, or, like Max and me, retired on the pension we'd fought so hard for). And if we weren't a Collective, were we really a Colony anymore? Or did we just keep up the Barn, the meetings, the Party lingo and jingo to put ourselves at ease about that new sundeck, new white Buick, new parquet floor, new and private everything?

I gulped my coffee. It wasn't just the Feds who were threatening the Colony. After all, who was taking it apart, piece by piece, with every new tchotchke bought with private money? Us, that's who.

I'd never thought of it that way before, but there it was. Yes, it's us who are dissolving us; not "them," whoever they may be. Us, good old us. Ha!

But who am I to criticize? I had my own house, and a private bank account, too: 108-54-9197. I loved those numbers; they seemed lucky, just because they were mine. I liked my private bank account, and I'm sure most of the rest of us did.

Most folks had already left the Colony, anyway. It was just us seven. Soon they'd all be gone, off to the suburbs, to join Wool Cap and the rest.

Or were the others, the brave remaining few, still committed? Was *I* the only one who didn't honestly give a damn about the Cause, the Struggle, the Party anymore? I sighed, finishing my coffee. I wasn't sure. Without Max, it was hard for me to figure out what I still believed. That had been Max's department.

Well, I knew I still loved my garden. And my kitchen. My eyes darted around the kitchen, taking stock. My kitchen, decorated in Party red. A square Russian clock with a red hammer-and-sickle face, a maroon slate floor, and brick red Formica counters. All that good red, home only to me and my tomato plants. No longer the Colony's.

A noise like a running faucet startled me. The boy! I'd forgotten all about the boy.

I looked back outside. He'd stopped digging to pee in the hole he'd dug.
He shook his thing off. It was a peachy pink, same shade as his nipples, only deeper. The head, hidden now under that little flap, seemed too large for the shaft. He didn't look at it as he shook. But oh, they were clever, whoever manufactured him, choosing pink, then applying it so liberally all over his body. It's hard not to love what's pink.

Good morning, ladies and gentleman. Eight forty-one, and it's gonna be another scorcher, clouds clearing by midday, reaching highs of one hundred in the city, a bit cooler in outlying areas. I didn't recall turning the radio on, but there it was, the morning announcer with his deep baritone. A comfort; with Max gone, I missed hearing a man's voice with my morning coffee. I always kept the radio set to 94.3 FM, my favorite station, the only decent station we could get out here. 94.3 FM, telling me the time and temperature.

Simon was digging in the dirt now, crouched on his hands and knees, scooping the earth with his palms. I should have stopped him, but I just watched, and then stopped watching. Out in Sylvan Lake, it was always a few degrees cooler than in the city, but the trees and the Lake and the tsuris made it more humid. Another scorcher, eh? Then today, I resolved, I won't go out without my hat. Today is a hat day. A perfect day for my orange straw.

I fished around in the coat closet for the hat, remembering how we met. When I saw the hat at May's Department Store, I knew it was mine. Such an unlikely color: pale orange, like sherbet. Tightly woven straw, the expensive Italian kind, with a curved top and wide brim. A cloche, they called it. French. And the trim! Who ever thought of feather trim? The dyed orange ostrich feathers were so tightly woven together around the brim that at first I thought it was fur.

The whole hat was too much. It reminded me of hats in those movies during the War, pushed over the forehead of a tough-talking broad who never once had to think about rationing. It was an old-fashioned hat, a little out-of-date even back when I bought it back in '48. But that silly cloche called to me, lumping my throat like the runt of a litter. Amidst all the white summer straws with sensible navy ribbons, I picked this meshugge hat.

I tried it on in the privacy of the lady's dressing room; I couldn't stand in the Summer Separates department of May's in this hat. I took a white silk shirt in, too, a plain blouse two sizes too large for me, with a prim Peter Pan collar designed for an office girl, so that the girl monitoring the dressing room wouldn't give me any nonsense about wasting a whole room to try on one measly hat. I held its brim, undid my bun, and placed it gently on my head.

It smelled like France. As I scrutinized myself in the mirror, I hesitated. It clashed with my red hair. But if I didn't take this poor hat home with me, it would never be worn. It would lie for months in the marked-down bin, like a young girl lying in bed, dreaming of her first lover.

At first I thought I'd take my cloche down to the Lake at the Colony, wear it with my black swimsuit with the white polka dots, but before I could even hold the image in my mind, I knew I could never wear such a rich lady's extravagance in front of the Colony wives. What would Elaine, or Mady, or even Gladys say to such a hat? Though everyone had the nice dress for Friday-night dances at the Barn, and a decent hat or two to wear on the train, a fancy-shmancy Continental cloche like this was unheard of at Sylvan Lake. It would have supplied a summer's worth of Colony gossip: "Did you get a load of Sylvia's hat? She looks like a fool. A bourgeois fool. That Sylvie; she always was a suspicious character, what with that rich sister and all." So the hat remained unworn, hidden in my closet behind my collection of broken hand bags and scuffed shoes.

But I'm getting sidetracked again. You don't want to hear about my hat! To continue:

On that day, the scorcher when we were to deed the Colony houses, I dug the cloche out of my closet. When I put it on, I was surprised at how light it was, how jauntily it perched on my head. It had a good brim, wide and light, and the trim weighted it nicely, so I suspected it would stay on even when I gardened.

I went outside with my hat tilted rakishly to one side. Simon was standing, stiff and straight, in the middle of the tomato plants again. His lovely feet were buried, ankle deep in dirt. When he stood very still, he blended in with the plants.

They made him too rubbery. His skin was probably derived from some rare white rubber plant forested in the depths of the jungle, out in Brazil, or Ceylon, or somewhere so remote only the FBI can land there in their single-prop jets. It's just a dirt road, really, the runway into the forest. Planes often crash into the majestic white plants, blinded by all that white.

Or maybe they're not really rubber plants; there's no English translation for their real name. They're relatives of ferns, but with thick watery leaves. The FBI boys just call them rubber plants, since they yield a fleshy, oily substance that can be used in all the ways that rubber is used.

The processing plant is on an island off the mainland, away from the thick "rubber" trees. It's a grim, faceless plant, smelling of sweat and coal, anonymous and ugly, like any other such factory in Detroit or Timbuktu. The workers are poor men, farmers, their hands callused thick from working the fields, their brown faces grayed with soot. They are grateful for the ship that sails them off from the mainland to the factory island to melt the leaves down until they turn to a plasticky goo, malleable and colorless. The rubber season only lasts a month; then it's back to the fields for the workers.

Quite a complicated process they go through to get such perfect skin, I thought, gazing at his pale arms. Do they make the scabs too, or are those real?

Or maybe he was a mix of materials, gathered from all four corners of the earth, assembled in a small dirty factory in Detroit. Perhaps other robots chose the materials. A robot made by robots.

Animal, mineral, or vegetable? I couldn't decide. His skin definitely had a rubbery aspect to it, though. I watched him dig in my garden, making odd marks in the ground with a stick, remembering the feel of his fingers in the pantry. His skin glowed, wet with perspiration.

Stop staring, I scolded myself. Stop watching. Go to the meeting. Ignore the boy, ignore the sun, get to the meeting and worry about your future, Sylvie, you old hussy you. But I couldn't.

In the garden, I stood behind him and touched his shoulder. "Hello?"

Simon scowled at me and turned his back.

"ZZZZssss. ZZZZssss."

Where was that sound coming from? I pulled him to face me and he didn't resist. It seemed to be emanating from him, but I couldn't locate it; I saw no hole or spout or point of origin. Just the boy, and the sound, together and not.

"Fine, just ignore me. Go ahead; kanoodle my nipples in the pantry, then mess up my garden with your piss and sticks; I don't give a damn," I shouted, "It'll all be gone soon, anyway, and then where will you be? Back at the plant? In a cushy desk job? On another mission?"

He crouched down, like a dog, cowering before a blow.

"Oh stop that, Simon. Jesus."

*

I made my way out of the garden to the driveway, breaking into a jog, running down Old Colony Road away from the boy, toward the Barn. I stood and looked back a minute, hoping he'd look, too. He was sitting in the soil, picking a scab, making it bleed.

My hat slipped as I marched. "Goddamn cloche," I cursed, pulling it back on. How dare they plant spies in my garden?

The brim dipped down over my left eye, turning half the world into an orange sea. You're not getting off this easy, I grumbled silently as I moved the brim back up, my legs marching down the road to the Barn at a Cossack's furious pace. You'll see, you little dirt-digging bastard. I'll make you speak. I'll open your mouth with my fingers, stretch it until the speech pours out. "Thank you," you'll say in a voice on the verge of change, gray blue eyes widening. "Thank you, my darling Sylvie." Or maybe I will catch your silence, my throat closing in solidarity with yours.

I slowed, standing in front of the Barn a minute to

catch my breath, wondering what your mouth was doing
at that very second in my tomatoes.

VI. Map, Plan, Man

Simon swallows and tastes cum. An hour ago a man was inside me, and now I'm sitting in some goddamned garden, he thinks without emotion.

Mother must be doing the files. Sunday night, so she'll be rushing to straighten things up for Monday morning. His stepfather leaves the bills and papers in a shapeless heap on the kitchen table on Friday night, and Monday morning takes them in a neat square pile back to the shop, all folded and filed. She even writes the checks for him, the fucking grease monkey. His stepfather the mechanic, black oil smeared between his bushy eyebrows. His stepfather the devil with a monkey wrench. At least Simon won't end up like him. He'd rather drown in the smelly sea.

Speaking of which, he's gotta find some water, soap, a shower, a beer. Simon swallows and tastes his own dry mouth.

*

Or maybe you didn't taste anything. Maybe you left when I left. Yes, you left the garden and went back to headquarters, a local Lewisboro farm, the inside gutted, walls lined with humming gray machines and test tubes. Zzzzsss. Or maybe you hid in the woods and went to sleep in your...hut? Pod? Capsule? Stepfather's home?

Or maybe you stayed. You sat in the dirt, picking your scabs, messing up my garden, tasting nothing at all.

*

Whatever you tasted, the fact remains that I came to the meeting late and sat in the back, where the kids had stored their props for the last May Day parade. Nobody had bothered to throw them out. "Solidarity!" said a giant cartoon cow painted on a cloth banner.

I leaned against a cardboard sign with "Freedom" painted on in a child's uneven orange scrawl. It was warm in the Barn, too warm for the lemonade passed around in Dixie cups. Ceiling fans moved the hot air from one side of the room to another. Sheppie's Barry from Brooklyn had already come and gone, taking Sheppie with him, but whatever he'd said seemed to have only increased the aroma of panic.

"What we need is a plan." Mady thumped her cane on the floor for emphasis.

"You want a plan? I'll give you a plan: go to Moscow! That's the only place they won't get you. We should scrap the whole damn thing and set up a new colony in Moscow!" Elaine didn't usually speak at meetings. Her specialty was gossip; she left the politics to Joe, but now even Elaine was a politico.

Joe chimed in, arms slicing the air, eyes wild. "In Russia they'll give us land. And factories, not just some old shmatte of a barn!" He chugged on his chin like he was milking an unwilling cow. I thought of your chin, its weedy blond wisps.

"Joey-boy, Joltin' Joseph. What, you want to have a heart attack already? Settle down. What we need here is solidarity, not a bunch of squabbles." Louie strode into the center of the circle, glowering. Joe sat back down, his new Colony shining in his eyes, so much better, so much more united than this uncomradely den of creeps. He pointed at Louie and mouthed the word "gonif" and everybody laughed.

Hands flew up, debate twirled in loud, smoky circles around me, and I ate my last licorice from the pack, fumbling for a tissue to wipe off the sticky red goo. But despite all the big talk of Moscow and Solidarity and a New Colony in Detroit, I could see plans forming in the eyes of the women as they squinted and blinked, speedy getaway plans brewing underneath each exasperated sigh. But the men, oy gevalt, the men. The smart ones were busy covering their asses, already scripting their chat with HUAC. The dummies were squabbling over the ruins: who gets the Barn? Who gets the lawnmower? On and on they bickered.

I looked at Gladys; she knew. *This is the end*: who will be the first to say it?

Well, it was me. "The Colony is mechuleh. Over! Why don't we face facts? We're not going to turn private and then just go on our merry way. As though the Feds won't notice that we're the same pinkos we always were!" Everyone looked at me. Sheppie was giving me the frown, eyes cold, arms crossed. I didn't care. "And no, Ellie, we're not going to Moscow. Moscow! To do what, join Uncle Joe's gulag?"

And what do you think happened next? Did the buck stop here? Did they stop squabbling and face the facts? Did they deny it?

Of course not. They kept right on.

"Of course, darling." Mady was the first to respond, smiling her gums at me. "Nobody expects us to go to Moscow, Sylvieyenkele, not youngsters like us, eh darling?" Everyone laughed. "But not to worry; the Party will take care of you. There's a nice place in Forest Hills for us single gals. Don't worry, mein tsatskele Sylvie. Sheppie, now who gets the nice rug we used to have here in the Barn? Remember that rug, the green one with blue trim?" And on it went. *Who gets the coffee urn. Who gets the lawn mower? I hear in Moscow you don't need lawn mowers; they know how to grow grass that never gets to be longer than an inch. I hear the gulag is a capitalist lie; Uncle Joe will take care of us all.*

The boy's mouth, the pink and pulse of it. Stop thinking of that, Sylvie you old slut, Max piped in; think of the Cause, the dishes unwashed in the kitchen, anything. Okay, tomatoes. Oy gevalt, my tomatoes. I pictured them waiting in my garden. The German Johnsons, Hughses, Green Zebras, Brandywines, Purple Cherokees—all the heirlooms are getting blight. I think it's because they're getting too much water. I won't water them today and see how they do. Or it could be the piss. The yellow clings to the tip; I'd felt it drip on my thigh, I—

"I have a proposal," Sheppie announced.

Proposals; these shmendricks always had proposals. That's why it took so damn long for us to build the Colony in the first place. Everything always had to be done by Committee; everyone on the Committee had his own proposal; everybody clung to his own precious proposal, so nobody ever made a goddamned decision. Even when we were building our houses, these houses that now we were so eager to abandon...

I drifted away from the meeting, the piss and tomatoes, into a light nap, back to my Sleeping House. "It looks like it's sleeping," I told Max, my first pronouncement after he'd finally ignored the damn Committee and finished putting up the walls and roofing. The second story drooped over the first floor like an old man falling asleep in an easy chair, head slipping down into his newspaper. Max built it right on top of the old bungalow. Me? I never saw so much as a sketch; I wasn't allowed to any of the meetings where everyone proposed. No ladies invited. We only got to come to one lousy meeting when Louie and the gang decided we should "Commit to the Cause, make the Colony a permanent fortress for the Revolution, winterize, turn all these shlumpy bungalows into livable houses. Workers deserve decent housing and fresh air year 'round. Am I right? So come on, you shtarkers, let's get the hell out of those damn cramped city apartments!" And a couple of weekends later there it was: a real house, however saggy and small it might be. The Sleeping House, or at least the sleepy foundation.

"When can we move in?" I begged.

"Patience, Sylvie, patience. There's still a lot of kutchkying around to be done with the electricity. I gotta meet with Louie and the boys about it; we got a bunch of proposals to consider. Just wait a few more months." More meetings! More arguments! More fershtinkener proposals! I wasn't patient. "Nu, Moishe Pupik! When will the Sleeping House be finished?" I nagged, for fourteen more months.

That year, on cold spring weekends, when Max

would head out early on the train to go work on the house, he'd yell over his shoulder, "I'm going to Sleep." Our little joke. After Max died, I never called our house by name again.

*

And here we all were again, drowning in another sea of proposals, only now Max was gone. Dead. I don't like that word, "dead."

I jolted awake, leaving Max in the Sleeping House.

"So Louie, you're saying we dissolve the Colony, but keep our houses?" Mady was frowning, her face a wrinkled globe.

From the one, many. It was the same old issue we were stuck debating again here: how could we each get to own our own, without losing the collective spirit of the Colony? Except now the answer seemed all too obvious: we couldn't. But that didn't stop everyone from yammering on.

I drifted off again, letting the words everyone was yelling out spill over me: *Feds. Dissolve. Ownership.*

From the many, one. It's a funny thing about ownership. You don't notice it. You think, now I'll get to have things my way, now I can fix the house up the way I please, now I can have everything just so. You don't think about the freedom you're losing. See, when you own, you're shackled: to your own choices, your taste, your mistakes. That unity business the Party makes so much of is true. But it's a collectivity of crap, flowing back up through everyone's identical toilets. Solidarity through shit!

From the one, many. That's what Joe always intoned. Do you know that until we built the Sleeping House, me and Max never spent a single night alone? In our apartment on Avenue J, we had a parade of cousins: Cousin Marty and his kids, then one of Marty's cousins, all sharing our single bedroom and kitchen. And then in the Colony, first we were single in the tents, along with everyone else, and then coupled in the bungalows, where you weren't allowed to lock the doors or close the windows, "To each according to his needs, from each according to his abilities." God how I hated that phrase.

Our quarters were too close not to share some other things. The Lake was the place for that; where else was there any privacy except at the Lake? In the bushes by the Lake, of course. That's how it started with Shep and me: one night, after a long meeting, he grabbed my arm and walked me to the Lake. I was wearing a new peach taffeta that everyone said complimented my hair, with a red satin sash tied at the waist the way all the girls did that summer. He led me by the arm, not kissing or kutchkying, just pulling me forward, leading, smiling his warm smile. My Sheppie; he had the sun in his smile back then. We joked about Joltin' Joe and his shmaltzy folk songs, about Bella tripping beside him as she danced in her high heels, but we knew what we were up to. At the Lake, Shep led me to a large maple and knelt. Hand between my legs, outside my dress, then inside, everywhere. I looked up through the trees, a sky of maple and midnight and felt my dress still on, sash tied tight. Only a year after I'd married Max it was. There were other times, years full of other times, but of course it's the first time that I remember best.

In the morning I slipped back to my bungalow, still in the peach taffeta. Max woke, and said nothing. If nobody was supposed to own any thing, how could you claim to own any one? That was our line back then, though nobody bought it.

*

"Joe, for chrissake, we don't have time to argue ideology." While I was daydreaming about kanoodling with Sheppie, Louie, practical Louie, was disagreeing with whatever Joe had just said. Louie looked exhausted, gray bags pillowing his eyes. "We gotta make a plan. We don't have time for this mishegas; they're moving in on us, and we gotta move fast. So let's vote on my proposal: do we go to Russia and start all over again, or do we stay and end up getting our asses kicked by some little Lewisboro red-baiting shtunk?"

Joe rubbed his chest hard, glaring at Louis. His shirt was sweated through. "Comrade, are you suggesting that we allow our class enemies to set our Colony's agenda?"

I couldn't stand it. My tomatoes needed to be caged, and there I was, listening to yet another stupid Colony squabble. Well, I'd had enough. I stood, hoping no one would notice my early departure. Time for tomatoes.

I flashed on Simon, naked among the tomatoes, and felt a little twinge of whatever happened in the pantry stir between my legs. Tomatoes, Sylvie, I thought fiercely: just worry about the tomatoes.

Tomatoes are tough customers. They're not like zucchini. Zucchini you just plant, water, and wait. Not so fast when it comes to tomatoes, buster. You've got a lot of work ahead of you. Staking and caging come first. Unstaked, the tomatoes topple the whole plant to the ground, the fruits rotting before they ripen. Uncaged, they stew in their own juices in the hot sun. But cage them too early, and your plants will grow weak, limbs breaking against the stake. Do it too late, and they'll fall, too lazy, accustomed to curving toward the ground, unable to tolerate the tardy discipline of the stake. Once each plant is staked, you have to craft a wire holding cell for each plant, a metal cage to keep it from falling back over itself, into the ground. Such klutzes! You've got a lot of work ahead of you, mister, if you want tomatoes.

"Comrades, tokhis oytin tish, or as my grandson Danny would say, put up or shut up! It's time to vote on those proposals," Mady stamped her cane once on each word. Today would be a good day for staking, I thought. With this crazy heat, I'll bet they're just about ripe enough to stake.

Without a word to Sheppie or the rest, I ran out of the Barn, and sweated my way up Old Colony Road back home.

I gathered a bunch of branches I'd been saving out of the garage, pulling my orange cloche down on my forehead to shield me from the sun, found a stale pack of licorice stashed behind the gardening tools, and set to work. Just as I got going, staking the first of the plants, the phone rang.

And then it was later. And I was in bed, alone with Simon. And I will tell you nothing of it.

VII. Strawberries, Rabbits

"Bunny?"

There's no story there; Shep calls me Bunny, and I don't object.

"Bunny? Hon-bun?" Half-asleep, sweat-soaked sheets twisted around me, I thought it was the phone, shouting me out of my bed.

I reached over to Simon, but he was gone. The pillows were full of him, sand-sweat smell, garden dirt plus lemons. I buried my face in his pillow, giving it a quick lick with my tongue.

"Buuuuuny? You home?"

By the third Bunny, I ambled to the door. Sheppie in my doorway, filling up the door frame.

"All right, all right. You don't have to yell already. What's your racket?"

"Strawberries. I'm in the strawberry racket, Bun, cornering the Lewisboro market, putting the squeeze on Little Al's fruit stand."

"Is that shtarker still around?" You had to wash Little Al's apricots with dishwashing soap, so dirty his hands were!

"He's a good boychik, a real worker, that Al." Sheppie examined his face in the mirror above the coatrack, gently stroking his beard as if he were caressing a lady's gloved fingers. "A real mensch."

"Please, Sheppie. Don't give me that." I stared up at the nose hairs. I look at Shep, I see nose hairs; he looks at me, he sees forehead. That's what happens when you're a half-foot shorter than your man. And I'm no shrimp boat, either, as you can see: five six and a half, tallest gal in the Colony. "And don't give me your damn strawberries, either; you know Gladys'll have a fit if she finds out." At least his nose was clean. A Polack nose, big and wide, but straight; some great aunt back in Lvov didn't run fast enough from the Cossacks, eh Sheppie?

"She wants for you to have them, Bun. From

Gladys." He thrust a mixing bowl full of strawberries and sour cream into my arms.

I flinched, wanting to thrust them right back at him. Gladys' strawberries he gives me! "Thank you, darling. And thank you to Gladys." I held the bowl to my tummy. The berries didn't look so good. Their skin was bruised, purpling like a woman with a drunken husband. "So. Nu, Sheppie? What brings you to my doorstep?"

"Bunny, I need your help. The papers. You remember the papers? Joe's been hocking me a tchynik about those damn papers," Sheppie explained, face tight and serious. "I know Max had 'em in here somewhere. So we gotta find them, and fast. He picked up a couch pillow, tossed it in the air, and dropped it. "Maybe under the pillow, heh heh."

A pillowful of Simon, my tongue on his cheeks, his little shmekele curled soft on his leg, above the scab, my hand pulling the scab, peeling it off like the shell of a shrimp, an onion, a pirate...

"Bunny? Are you listening? This ain't a joke. I need the damn papers, pronto Tonto. I got plans to get the hell out of this ferkakte place and start another colony north of Moscow. Do it right this time, no private property, no monkey business. We'll get rid of all the class traitors like Joe and his gang, and start a real workers' cell."

He lowered his voice even more, so I could hardly hear him. "But first I gotta sort out all these goddamn papers, sell off the joint, and leave clean. I don't want no problems from Immigration. " His chin was red from all the beard-pulling. Getting a little anxious, eh Sheppie boy?

"Yeah, yeah. What papers is it you need again? You know how I am about paper." I led him into Max's study, eager to get him out so I could find Simon, touch his rough knees, soft thighs, dirty toes. It was just like how I used to want Sheppie, risk Gladys' or Max's glare just to get a glimpse of him any way I could. And now I just wanted Sheppie out, and Simon in.

"The incorporation papers, Sylvie," Shep said,

eyes darting around the room looking for... spies? boys? turncoats? papers? Something about his eyes gave me a funny feeling. That blue, that ring of gold on the left, where had I seen it before? I squinted, but I didn't put the pieces together. Not then.

Sheppie bent down like he was telling a small child a secret, cupping my ear with his hand. "Help me out here, Bunny." He'd never have come except for the papers. It was them that made his mouth so wet. "They should say May 6, 1930 on the top. Or maybe May 7; I think we didn't get around to filing until the next morning. Yeah yeah, it was the seventh, I'm sure of it. We was a bunch of lazy schlemiels back then, wasn't we, Bunny?" Sheppie and his mouth: two different creatures. Such a talker, his voice believing itself, smooth as a radio announcer's, but just look at that mouth! A liar's mouth, a hangman's lips. That's what Mama said, at least. And I believe her.

"It's a green file, I think. With a tan label. You remember, Bunny? Sure you do. I gotta get 'em and burn 'em." He grinned, pulling his beard hard. Getting a bit nervous, Sheppieleh? "We got everything else wrapped up, but we gotta have the papers."

I knew exactly what he was after. The Green Papers, we called them, on account of the color of the file we kept them in. Max had drawn them up, since he was the best writer on the CCC. Somehow, the Green Papers never made it out of our house to the Barn, where they belonged. That's my Maxie: always hoarding. All Comrade This and Comrade That on the surface, but underneath it all, you were a stingy old capitalist momzer, clinging to whatever your paws could hold, now weren't you?

Ah Maxie. Did they put you up to it? Did you leave me with the papers, just so I would get nailed? No, I don't believe it. You were a bastard, but not a traitor. Though now, who knows? In here, anything seems possible.

But no more editorializing. Back to the Tale of Sheppie, Simon, and the Strawberries:

After an hour of tearing my house up, Shep gave up his search for the Green Files. "Guess Maxie-boy took them to the grave," he scowled. I glared, mock-shocked, then laughed, thinking of Max six feet under, clutching the damn file to his cold chest.

The grand search over, we went back to the kitchen to have some coffee. I was distracted. Those eyes, what was it with those eyes?

"You got company, Bunny?" Simon sat on my kitchen floor, shirtless, trousered in baggy tan pants, cinched with a big black belt. It gave him a girl's waist.

"Rose's?" Sheppie asked.

I didn't answer.

"You Rose's brat?" Sheppie asked with a grin.

Simon looked away, scratching his arm. Another scab.

"No," I answered for him. "One of the Feld boys. He's visiting from the City; I said I'd watch him while the Felds close up their house."

"Another one? Goddamn rabbits, those Felds. Hey, kiddo. I'm Shep Goldstein. And you're?"

Simon blushed, pushing his hair behind his ear like a girl. I could see the kids making fun of him at school, repeating the gesture, "Look, I'm Simon."

Shep smiled his coldest smile. "What's the story, buddy?"

"He's deaf," I stage-whispered, as if a deaf boy could hear.

"Ohhhh. Yeah, Gladys told me about him." Such a liar, that Sheppie.

But I can lie, too. "Deaf and dumb. Can't even say his own name. But he answers to it, like a goddamned dog."

Sheppie stared at Simon. "Have I met you before?"

I laughed. "Shep, enough already. The kid's a retard. Give him a break, will ya?" Simon lunged toward Sheppie, as though he were going to take him down, but then dodged right, and ran into the bathroom, slamming the door shut. I watched his naked back and trousers disappear. What do they call those pants, the tan kind made of sailor cloth?

"Jheesh. Kids these days."

"Well, he's got a tough load. Being a retard and all. Have a heart, Shep." Something with a *k*?

Sheppie smiled. "Oh Bunny, I got lots of heart. Too much heart, that's my problem, right?"

I looked away, not smiling back. Kickies? No, that's not right. "Well, you got too much of something, that's for sure.

"I guess I better be going and let you get back to playing nursemaid here." He paused. "So Bunny, I hear that you're selling this place and movin' in with Rosie?"

I wasn't listening; I thought I heard Simon moving outside, a rustle in the garden. Did he sneak out the bathroom, run out the front door, and slip into the garden while we were sitting here yakking about him? Such glorious soiled knees, like earth was sprouting out of his pores. Or maybe it was just paint, some waterproof brown gunk you boys cooked up in the lab.

"Bunny?"

I looked at Sheppie. What the hell are you doing here? Oh, something about a list. No, not a list; a file, that's right. "Sorry Shep. I'm all fagged out from this heat. What were you saying?"

"You movin' in with Rose, I hear?"

"No! Who told you that?" I frowned; Sheppie should know I'd die, vote for Ike, and wear a yarmulke before I'd move in with my sister. "I'm staying. What about you and Gladys?"

"Oh, we're planning on joining another colony in Russia." I looked deeper into Sheppie's grin, to see if his golden eye was shining the way it did when he was lying. No; it was fool's gold, no glisten. "In the north, near Moscow. With no Feds to cock it all up." Oy veh, not more babble about Moscow! I couldn't wait to get rid of him, to find Simon cinched in those pants, those kick, kack— "But I swear Joe or Mady was telling me last night that you'd sold the house and were on your way to Jersey next month."

"Well they told you wrong. I'm staying. They'll have to cart me away in my gardening pants."

We laughed together at that prospect as I led Shep out the front door.

"You be good, Bunny. Don't go talking to no strangers." Khakis: that's what they call them.

I went out to the garden, but Simon was gone. It had rained during the night; the earth was smooth. No high arches, no toe prints.

I pretended to weed, thinking of the pants. Who chose them? Simon in the store with his mother, trying them on. He wants blue jeans, to go with his leather biker jacket. She chooses the khakis; "so nice with that blue sweater." What would she look like? Blue eyes, nervous smile. Pinched face, small features. A bottle blonde: Marilyn Monroe with a sick headache.

He models the blue jeans for her first, turning three-hundred-sixty degrees like a model. "Oh Simon, you look like a hood!"

In the dressing room he models them for himself, arms crossed, eyes squinting, his thing hard, visible through the blue jeans. In the full-length mirror, he looks like a man.

"Try the khakis, honey."

He tries on the khakis, still hard. They're two sizes too big. He turns his hand into a belt, cinching the waist. "There. I look like a nerd. Are you happy?"

She laughs. "You'll grow into them. You can use your belt, the one Uncle Frank gave you."

He can hear her at the counter as he changes back into his old pants; they're not jeans, but at least they're black. "We'll take the khakis."

Or perhaps they're not yours. They gave them to you at the plant. Here, take these, the man in the gray suit says, handing you a plaid satchel with two large pairs of khakis inside. They're theirs, threaded with wires, the tan a perfect camouflage for a microphone.

FINK

Even the pants have ears, eh Simon?

VIII. Pens, Cars

Why did I paint these walls blue? I awoke in a nameless hour that night, cold and critical, frozen bones inside boiled flesh, looking up at the blue ceiling, a dead sky. Why don't they call them "hot and cold flashes"? Simon was beside me in the bed, asleep in a thin sheet, unperturbed by my freeze-and-fry.

I put on two cotton undershirts, gardening pants, thick socks, a cotton sweater—Max's fishing sweater. I dug around the room in the dark, hating the walls, my frozen fingers, this night. I opened the top drawer of my bureau and pulled out some pens, as if I could draw myself a blanket.

More clothes, an old blue shirt from the J street days, the orange cloche, leather gloves for snowplowing. Still cold. A wool blanket, pilled and smelling of mothballs. A thick pair of gardening socks. But I was still frozen, an ice skeleton, skin just a dusting of snow. I sank back into sleep, worrying about the walls.

*

Sylvia.

He didn't say my name, but I heard it anyway, pushing me awake. *Sylvia, Syl Sylvie Sylvia.*

Simon was lying on his stomach in my bed, making a miniature fort out of my pens on the sheets. The fort kept falling.

I sat up, facing him, and took off all those layers. An idea formed. A solution to all our problems. "Simon, do you want to learn how to write?"

Yes, he nodded.

I got out of bed and grabbed one of the pens, and tore a half-blank page from Max's yellow pad of meeting minutes still lying on the bureau. "Here. I'll show you how. Penmanship was my best subject."

He took the pen and paper and started scribbling

furiously, **ABD GHDK DFG DSBD SGYZ ZZZZZZZ.**

"You know your alphabet then, eh Simon?"

Of course, his eyes rolled, *stop treating me like I'm seven.*

"Let's try something else." ***Simon loves Sylvia,*** I wrote neatly on the paper. "Now, see that snaky letter there? That's an *S*, Ssss for Simon. And Sylvia! See? Ssss. *S*. Here, you try."

Simon took the pen and threw it across the room. Gently, he pushed my chest down, and dug his nail across my back. I twisted around to see.

S.

The letter disappeared back into my skin like sky writing as we read it.

And then, **Simon lorves Mrs. Ebelman**, you scratched, the extra *r* nestled against the *v*, the *d* flipped backwards into a *b*. For a moment we could read all the letters.

Well, then! You could write after all. Twisting around, I grabbed your finger and held it up close to my eyes.

"No."

Did you say it, or did I? It was my voice, but I swear it came from your mouth. Your lips were dry, peeling in the corners from too much sun. Your fingers curled in a baby clutch, mouth open, not quite reaching a perfect *o*. A crowd of fingers grabbed at my breast like yentas at a yard sale.

I couldn't kiss you. Your face was too symmetrical, your features too even, like a turncoat snitch, a rubber boy, a writing robot. I watched your lips pucker, but I didn't pucker back.

Your mouth sat in the center of your face, like the pit of a green peach in a winter market. It was probably part of the plan: let's make a face based on the statistical norms of all thirteen-year-old boys born in—what year would that have been, '39? '38? No, it was '40. 1940. A good year for the Colony. Not such a good year for me; that was the February I lost the baby. Pissed him right into the toilet. A stream of blood, ripping, pain, a soft plop, and that was it. I don't remember much about it; just running like a madwoman up Danger Road to Sheppie's in my nighty, terrified that Max would find out, then a rip and the bloody plop.

I released your face. The lips unpuckered into a silly asymmetrical smile, one side higher than the other.

"I, do, I, love you, Silly Simon." I sang; I don't remember the tune. The sides of your mouth curled into a giggle, Shirley Temple dimples on either end. We both laughed. I was hoping a word would slip out of you.

Your lips pursed, an old-lady tightness gripping them together. The Prince of Pouts. Up this close, I could see they were heavily lined, too many lines for a young boy's lips. Perhaps all those crevices were especially engineered to collect my spit, store it for analysis back in their laboratories, days or weeks or years in the future. I pursed my own lips back at you, feeling the muscles tense up, and brought my mouth to yours. I let my muscles go slack. Yours stayed, pursed and tight. Our first real kiss. (Whatever happened in the pantry didn't count.)

The phone rang, paused, and rang again.

Goddamn phone!

We listened, clenched together in the awkward kiss. A tire screeched, and the phone began again. Ring pause ring. Nebraska.

Were they calling to see if you'd made it inside? Did some low-level CIA goon in an ugly brown suit and matching hat cross off "Call Edelman residence. If phone is unanswered, assume agent has penetrated" on a long list of things to do before his lunch break at noon? Was it you?

Sssszzz, Ssssz, ring, ring. As the phone rang, the szzzzing began.

Was that it? Did the phone bugs activate some secret machine inside you?

Or was it just a coincidence? Maybe it was just Rose, ringing me up, to let me know what time she would be coming tomorrow.

SSSzzz. No, Rose knew better than to keep ringing.

Szzzz. Szzzzzzzz. I sat up in bed, wondering what to do.

To listen to someone listening is a queer thing. How do you respond? How do you act normal, not "act" at all, not tip off the listener that you, too, are listening?

We were baffled. We knew how to talk back to management, to the coppers in a rally, even to the landlord on rent day. To fight their words with ours. But how do you respond to ears? The listening machine has no thoughts, and nothing to say. It only listens, catching each stutter, each pause, the clearing of your throat as you gather your thoughts. What finks those fershtunkener machines are. All ears, no brains, but ready to repeat every stinking word they hear back to headquarters. Isn't that right, Simon? Eh?

*

As I kissed you back, I tried to locate the listening. At least the infiltrators had to sit through our boring meetings with us, drink our stale coffee in plastic cups, misquote Marx. At least they had to speak. But these ears were silent.

My tongue searched down your throat, prying open those dry lips, but I couldn't find anything but phlegm.

He pulled away and stared back at me, not talking or kissing back, gray blue eyes hard and opaque, no mirrors of the soul there, buddy.

I stared back. What eyes.

"Simon?"

Of course he didn't answer. But he curled his lips into a snarl, the look a kid gives his mother when he's about to say something fresh, and I saw it: Sheppie's eyes!

Pale gray blue, with a touch of yellow ringing the left iris. Shep's eyes, Sheppie Goldstein's eyes, stuck smack in Simon's head! How could it be?

I looked more closely. Yes, they were Sheppie's, all right. No doubt about it. The shape, that cold gray stare, those lids: Shep's. And the gold ring around the left iris was the dead giveaway.

Was Shep in on this whole business? Did he take the early train to make a quick trip to a factory buried deep in northern Queens, a morgue-like place? It's a delicate operation, eye-plucking; the machine can scoop them out, but it takes a team of surgeons, the very best, to sew an eye to a foreign face. I could see Sheppie's mouth twisting in pain as it leaves the socket, the left one with the yellow spot, oh how he groans, Christ motherfucking CHRIST!

But wait. I'd seen Sheppie just yesterday, eyes intact, seen him *in the same room with the boy*. Yet these were definitely Sheppie's eyes, resting calmly inside Simon's head. I spread the left one open with my fingers, like an ophthalmologist. The boy allowed the inspection, smiling as I gaped into his eyes.

It's Shep. Shep's. But that's impossible. His eyes can't be here and there, in Sheppie and Simon. So they... *borrowed* Sheppie's eyes? And then, what? Somehow replicated them? Harvested a twin? Borrowed the eyes for an hour to do the deed, but then returned them to the rightful owner?

I pressed my face to Simon's, eye-to-eye. Did he see what Sheppie saw? See me through Shep's jaded eyes? My own eyes blurred. Easy, Sylvie girl, don't lose your head now, I commanded myself silently in Max's patient-angry voice. Don't go nutso on me.

I closed my eyes for a moment, and opened them. Stay calm.

The boy blinked, giving me a perplexed look. I couldn't remember Sheppie ever looking so confused. So—what's the word? Feckless? That's it. A word from Mrs. Reingold's Advanced Senior English. Remember her, Sheppie? Simon? Is Mrs. Reingold in your files? Scratched on your retina? Her sheer white blouses, heavy black shoes? Of course you won't tell me that, now will you? To proceed:

I hesitated. Simon glared a Sheppie glare at me.

"Sheppie, is that you?"

He stuck out his tongue at me. Now what was that supposed to mean?

I decided to change the subject; obviously the direct approach wasn't working.

"Juice?" I asked, the word surprising me as it glided from my lips.

He nodded, giving me a suspicious look. After all, old ladies are known to serve odd fluids: prune juice, thick and shit-colored; tomato juice, like runny spaghetti sauce served in a cup; and apple juice, the eternal yellow apple juice of yentas throughout the universe, tasting of whatever it sits next to in the refrigerator.

I brought Simon three glasses of juice: tomato, apple, and grape. I placed them on the nightstand beside the bed, and watched him eye each glass. They're girl's eyes, at any rate.

"Girl's eyes," I said to Simon as he contemplated the juices. That's what I told Sheppie the first time we made love.

Simon's eyes flickering over each glass, not settling on one.

Those were Shep's eyes, there in my kitchen, there in Simon's head. I took the grape, hoping he'd follow my example and choose one, but in my haste I almost knocked the apple over. "Shit!" I yelled, thinking "Shep" but turning him to shit on my tongue.

Simon rolled his Shep eyes, disgusted. Kids don't like it when old ladies swear. But at least he didn't run.

"Here," I said, gesturing toward the glass of apple juice. He stuck his tongue out at me, and I grabbed him, held his head, opened his mouth, stroked my tongue beneath his tongue, forgetting all about Max, Sheppie, Sheppie's eyes.

Ssssszzz.

Ssszz, Ssssszz, coming from under his tongue.

I kissed you, wed your tongue. Could it be taught to speak? Maybe they gave you a slug tongue on purpose. They didn't want you smooth-talking the enemy; "Better no words than the wrong words," some mustachioed big shot decreed in an orange-carpeted conference room. Szzzzz. I felt it in your chest, the noise, the motor of the noise.

You pulled away and wiped your mouth, grinning. What the hell was I doing, anyway, French-kissing some strange boy? Even if he was a robot. Or a spy. Or Shep.

We smiled at each other, suddenly shy. I'll do nothing, I decided. I'll pretend I don't notice the eyes, the sound. Two can play this silent observer game. I'll watch like he watches, and see if they're really Shep's, if he's a spy, if his tongue can talk. I'll see what I see. But what to do now, right now?

You kept smiling and crouched on the floor, making digging motions with the eraser end of a pencil in my rug. SSSSSzzzzz Sssszzz. The sound was getting louder. I could tell you were bored; another minute, and you'd be darting away again. I looked around the room for an enticement.

The juice! Saved by the juice!

"Well, which one do you want?" I asked casually, pointing at each like a waitress. The buzzing stopped.

Simon pointed at the grape, and I held it under his chin and he drank it down.

Only a little spilled on his chest. And by the time we reached the bottom of the glass, we had it down to a science: I knew exactly how to angle the glass so that he could swallow without choking.

He said nothing as he finished. He was splattered in juice, streaks of grape dripping down his chest.

I didn't clean up. And I didn't try to touch under his tongue again, or ask about the Shep eyes. Instead, I pulled out a pack of red licorice that I'd hidden under the rug. "Candy? They're my favorite. Red licorice, like they have over in Spain," I offered. He took.

He diddled with the wrapper, folding it into tiny pieces and then unfolding it as I talked. Such noise that wrapper made!

Then, instead of eating the licorice, he pretended to smoke it, puffing on the end with exaggerated gestures. I puffed mine, too.

Distractions, we need distractions. Something to keep his attention. But what? I know: I'll tell him about the Colony. He won't even know I'm watching. He'll think I'm giving him the goods, telling him some top-secret Party dirt. "It's funny—I wasn't even so hot on joining at first. Sure, I went with Bella and the girls every weekend on the bus for a little fresh air, but all the constant bickering about politics just drove me nuts. It was like being back at the shop!"

I chomped down the rest of my licorice, and beamed at him. It's Sylvie the Spy now, my Simon-Pie. Ha! He was puffing and digging, making eraser marks on my rug in no discernible pattern. I pulled out more licorice, and gave him one, pretending to light it up. He accepted it, looking bored. He scratched a scab below his left knee. A fresh one, with a red aureole orbiting the blue center like the rings of a distant planet. I took a licorice for myself, pretending to light mine off his. He giggled as I pressed our licorices together, inhaling.

I talked. I told him all sorts of useless garbage, just what they'd expect from an old party bag! "...and then there was that constant singing. What is it with Party folks, eh Simon? They can't go five minutes without warbling about Joe Hill. Feh! I never liked those damn labor songs; I prefer the Negro spirituals, myself." I exhaled loudly on my licorice cigarette for emphasis. I never was a smoker, but I've always liked the way women look when they smoke in the movies, like elegant machines designed for the act of smoking.

Simon was losing interest; he'd finished his licorice. He wandered around my bedroom, rummaging through all the junk scattered around my bed. But I kept going.

"But then I met Max, and I knew I was here for good. He was hell-bent on turning Sylvan Lake into a real farm, where we could make it all with our own labor, our own two hands. That was one of his lines: 'We gotta be able to make it all with our own two hands.'"

I rambled on, telling him all about Max, the fascists in Spain, the fascists in Washington, the foibles of the Party, of Sheppie, Gladys, Joe, and Rose: lots about Rose and her schemes for me.

"She wants for me to move to some godawful ranch house in New Jersey. With no garden! And all those stinking capitalists crawling all over the place. Can you imagine?" I grabbed his shoulder and stared straight into his bleary Sheppie eyes. "Can you?"

No answer. He twisted out of my grasp. He went to a corner, where I had old issues of *Freiheit* piled up. I stopped talking, and walked over to observe.

"Simon? What are you doing?" I couldn't tell what his system was, but he seemed to have one. He carefully scanned the front page of each paper, placed it into a pile, examined the pile carefully, and then moved the paper from one pile to another. His Shep eyes were glowing, narrowed in thought.

"What are you doing?" Was he looking for something?

With grape juice still splattered across his chest, he stopped his sorting and rose from the piles of papers. Dropping the towel, he marched, Red Army–style, hup two, out of my bedroom, into my kitchen, toward the sliding-glass door. In his hand was the Green File. I followed in lockstep. "What have you got there?"

He stuck his tongue out, stained magenta from the juice and candy, and pushed me away. And out he ran, down my driveway, taking a left on Old Colony Road, off to who knows where.

I drank the two other glasses of juice, apple and then tomato. What else could I do?

IX. Pirates

Simon is tired. He's been on the run for only a few days, he's not even sure how many, but on the run it's a dog's life, and should be measured in dog-years. His fingers worry his chain as he ponders the blue Chevy. It's parked on the shoulder of the forked road. "Old Colony Road," reads one sign in tiny cursive letters. "Danger Road," reads the other. That's a good one.

The window isn't rolled up all the way, so it's easy to get in. Simon sits in the driver's seat. Now what? He can picture his stepfather laughing at him, his whiskey cheeks reddening. "Look at you! Livin' like a bum in some goddamn car." When will his stepfather discover that his satchel, bandanna, and new khaki pants are missing? He'll miss them more than he'll ever miss Simon, that's for sure.

It's hot in the car, worse than outside, even after he's rolled all the windows down. Hobo Trick #14: If you roll all the windows all the way down, from a distance it looks like they're rolled up.

He turns the steering wheel aimlessly. What now? It's been a hundred dog-years since he slept a full night. He could get in the back seat, bundle up his clothes for a pillow, and get a good night's sleep. He checks the glove compartment: a box of throat lozenges, a map, and two dollars in change. He pockets the money and the map, and eats one of the lozenges. Menthol, disgusting.

It's not stealing, he can imagine telling a cop. I'm borrowing, just until I get back to the city and find a job. Like that guy, who was it, Captain Cook? The one who stole from the rich and gave to the poor. Yeah, I'm that pirate, brother. Except I'm the poor. Ha! Simon crunches the candy wrapper and slumps down.

It's funny: he doesn't even remember leaving. Just his stepfather slapping him right across the temple, slurred curses burbling out of his mouth. He sees his head recoiling from the blow, and next he is on the highway, heading the hell out of Lewisboro, running into the night and the world and this car.

What now? Sleep. Here? They could come; a family of four, taking the car for a spin into town to get ice cream cones. But it's dusk, and it's boiling; who's gonna bother to go out on a hot night like this? He turns his body towards the east so the sunrise will wake him. There must be some food around here, kitchens or gardens or something. Fresh peas, string beans, and baked potatoes, oh yeah, potatoes with butter melting into the flesh. Gotta find some grub tomorrow, Simon thinks as he drops into sleep and dreams of a one-eyed pirate serving him a giant pot roast with buttered baked potatoes.

*

Maybe I don't have the details exactly right—it could have been a father, not a stepfather giving you the strap but yes, that's the gist of it. You could be a runaway, sure.

But what about the SSSzzz sound? How about the Shep-eyes?

*

In the factory, they don't bring him to life. That's later. "Assemble first, activate later," instructs a memo from the big boss. The mechanic shrugs; whatever you say, Boss. But he can't resist testing him out. What harm could there be in that? Besides, you really don't want to wait until he's already at headquarters to find the bugs in him. Bugs in him—get it? Ha ha ha. The mechanic swallows down wrong on a cup of styrofoam coffee as he laughs: bleh.

There's no switch to flip; it only works that way in the movies. Here's how it works: when you insert the eyes, a set of electrical connections is made, and then in four hours, he comes to "life." Like magic, but slower. They worked hard to make those eyes, Christ yes. Copying the eyes of the ringleaders—what a stroke of genius! As he twists the eyes in, the mechanic lets himself feel tired for the first time in days. "Go get 'em, Simon!" He looks at the boy, eyelids shut, and closes his own.

*

Well, that's a possibility. I'm sure I don't have every detail right, but that seems as likely as anything else.

Boy or man? Man or machine? Shep or Simon?

You still won't tell.

Angel or demon? Dog or cat?

So I'll just keep going.

*

Rose.

She's the next thing I remember.

*

Rose didn't come on time. I brewed and iced some black tea, set out dark seedless rye with cream cheese, turned the kitchen fan on high, and waited. It was the next day; I hadn't seen the boy since the business with the juice.

Three o'clock, then four, four-fifteen, and still no Rose.

I walked over to the stove, and stared at my hair reflected in the metal oven door. A streak or two or ten of gray ran through it, but still, good red hair. I bent down so that I could see my whole body reflected. Surprise! Thighs. They lolled over my knees. I bent down farther, and it only got worse, the flesh bunching up under the skin like a misplaced petticoat. You look like hell, Sylvie, I could hear Max say. Not like in the old days, when I was the envy of the Colony: muscular yet slender, bronzed, a good strong worker, yet still such a beauty, they all said, what with the red hair and all. Nothing like the heifer looking back at me in that stove-mirror! But at least my hair kept its color, with just a sprinkle of salt and pepper. Well-seasoned, eh, Maxie?

Goddamn Rose. She was just gonna come and criticize. "You're letting your looks go, Sylvie," she'll carp. "Getting a bit zaftig there, eh Sylvie?" To hell with you, Rose.

I combed my finger through my hair and drank some of the tea, giving the coffee a break for once. Rose with her banana-colored mix-master, I-Like-Ike butter dish, clamwich-filled summers at the Jersey Shore. "Don't you know what a clamwich is, Sylvie? What the hell do they feed you out at that pinko Colony, huh? *Red* lobsters!?!" She was always one for the corniest puns.

How did I end up with such a momzer of a sister? Mama a Red Russian, Papa a Trotskyite, even the uncles and cousins all solid rank-and-file, and then Rose. Rose the Republican. Rose the Bourgeois Bottle Blonde. Rose the Blue-Light Special. Ha!

5:10, 5:15: I watched the hammer and sickle show me how late Rose was.

But she still has my nose. She can't throw out that. She's got the Margolin nose, a straight line down, and then a big curve before the tip. Don't give me that "she can get her nose done" bupkes; no amount of surgery could rid her of that Margolin honker.

I stared out at my garden and tried to think of Rose's nose, our nose. But instead, Simon's hands swam back to me. Such lovely hands. (I won't tell you anything about them. A language that allows for banana butter dishes should never describe such fingers.) Simon kneeling in the soil, that old-man stoop, one hand fingering the weed of beard. Such hands.

I sat silent, waiting for Rose, and let his hands fold together in my head. As she brings news of the world, the mix-master, her youngest son's kindergarten, I'll pretend I'm watching Simon's hands, I decided. I'll feel them inside me, fingers lacing together, Shep-eyes closed.

I glanced outside. The light was fading, giving the tomatoes a dramatic blue black backdrop. 5:45 already.

The garden needed mulching, it was almost

dinnertime, and goddamn Rose still hadn't arrived! I was about to remind Max to mulch the garden before I remembered he was gone. Finally free of Rose and her red-baiting. *Rose.* Just the word would make his eyes roll. Would Simon hate her, too?

I tried to fuss with the bread, rearrange the teacups. Look busy. Pretend you're getting ready for Rose.

*

"Syyyyyyyylvie!" Rose's voice ripped up the driveway. "Nu? When the hell are those Colony commies going to pave the road already? It's like the Stone Age around here! I got lost three times just trying to find the turnoff."

Rose hadn't brought bagels, no. Just piles and piles of brochures, as many as she could fit under her thick arms. As we sipped the tea and spread cream cheese thick over the seedless rye, out it poured: the pitch. "Levittown would be perfect for you. The houses are twice the size of this dump, and they even have a recreation center, just like the Barn!" I nodded, fingering the glossy brochures. *Great Neck: A Family Kind of Town. Greenport: Champagne Living on Soda Pop Budgets! Teaneck, Your Town of Tomorrow.* Not my tomorrow, Rosie.

In the garden, a rustle. Was it him? Was he watching us, recording? I tried to look out of the corner of my eye so that Rose's eyes wouldn't follow mine.

"The rates are reasonable, and if you have any trouble selling this ferkakte heap, we'll give you a little loan. What, you're too good to take a little help from your family? You've got to be reasonable, Sylvie. You're getting on, you know. At fifty-three, who needs all this trouble, right, Sylvieleh? Even Max-God-rest-his-soul wouldn't have wanted for you to suffer. And frankly, we don't want no trouble, either. Nu, Sylvie? This is serious business, darling..." She always brought up my age when we had the Move to the Suburbs talk. As if getting to the suburbs first had finally made her the oldest. Rose the Protector, the one to stake out the property values and public schools. Rose the Rescuer, here to save her aging sister from the dirty Commies. Rose the Reliable.

"Right, Rosie." Usually, a compliant "Right, Rosie" and a nod or two shut her up, and she'd move on to the photos of Hesh and the boys and a vivid description of the latest addition to the banana appliance family. But this time she was unstoppable, an uncorked bottle of bad advice.

"Things are changing, Sylvie. It's time to grow up already. We don't want any trouble. We can help you; Heshie's got a cousin in the real estate business. You can always depend on family." Each platitude led her back to her main theme: Move to Levittown. Move to Teaneck, or Great Neck, or some other goddamn neck.

She grasped my hand, like they do in the movies, "Sylvie, don't be a fool. This is serious."

I nodded. My eyes trailed away from the kitchen, out into the garden.

"I'm not kidding this time, Sylvie. Things are getting worse."

A trickle of yellow wound its way between two tomato plants. Simon!

Was he taping us? Was every word of Rose's suburb babble imprinting its whine upon some special magnetic tape lodged way up in his head? Were his hands still as soft as yesterday? As they were in the pantry? I could feel my nipples hardening beneath them, his mouth closing in.

"What's this?" Rose picked up the satchel, and waved it at me. Simon's satchel, in Rose's hands! I squelched the impulse to snatch it away from her.

"Oh, I've been having a Lewisboro boy help me with the weeding," I improvised. I was getting good at this. "He must've left it." I did snatch it away from her, resting it on my lap.

Rose rolled her eyes. "See Sylvie, if you was in Jersey, you wouldn't need to bother with gardening. We'd set you up with a nice green lawn, and I could get little Stevie to mow it for you for free." I pictured Simon naked on a tractor, mowing a green lawn.

*

Finally it was over. Leaving a shiny sea of brochures, she got back in the white Buick and drove back to the banana kitchen. Her car moved slowly, like an overfed fish. "Call Me," she said in a grave tone, underlining each word with a squeeze of my hand. I followed her out the driveway, and watched the car swim away.

I put the satchel away in the pantry and walked straight into the garden. The puddle of yellow had left a dark brown stain between the two tomato stakes. There were no footprints this time, but he'd left behind a faded peach undershirt. I draped the shirt over the arm of the kitchen chair. The sunset made the plastic seat look molten. I picked his shirt up and sniffed. It smelled like laundry powder and sweat, neither scent canceling out the other. No lemon.

X. Khakis

After Rose left, I found you in the garden asleep, lying flat on your back, squashing my zucchini. The sunset hung over us hot and bloated, a real complainer. To hell with zucchini; I got too many anyways, I thought as I poked your hairless chest with my bare feet until you startled awake.

I couldn't help but smile as you opened your bleary Shep-eyes and gave me a confused grin. My Simon, my sweet Simon-pie. Rose and Max and the rest all vanished in the flash of your grin.

You were dirty again, and shirtless, with that pair of baggy men's trousers falling off your waist, tan khakis several sizes too big for you. A working man's pants.

"Whose trousers did you steal?" I asked, poking you in your skinny ribs with my big toe. You giggled, a light girlish laugh, giving me a peek at my favorite tooth, the front one with the chip on it.

"Get up, silly Simon." You lay on your back in my garden, crushing my snap peas and scratching an itch on your bare elbow, ignoring my command. I spied your balls pressed against your tan trousers, twitching like mouse ears. Small balls, a surprise, what with such a large member!

"C'mon, Simon Pieman. The old yenta left. You know, my sister Rose. She's gone. You can come back in." You lay there, looking up at me, grinning, not moving, of course not speaking.

So I picked you up and carried you in, cradling you awkwardly in my arms, the blushing bridegroom carrying his gal across the threshold. You didn't resist. In fact, you giggled, delighted with my struggle. You were almost my height then, five feet six inches. An equal match.

In the bathroom, I took off your pants and weighed you on the old scale, Max's scale, from back when he was trying to beef up for the Lincoln Brigade. It's a dark charcoal gray, the sort where you move the knob up and down, one thirty-five, thirty-seven, no, thirty-six, until the dial rests exactly at midpoint. You didn't resist; you seemed as curious as I was to discover your weight.

"One-sixteen, Mr. Simon Pieman Fancy-Pants," I pronounced, pointing at the dial. You furrowed your brows, snorted, and hopped off the scale. Before I knew it you were grabbing me in your arms, wrestling to get me on.

"Oh no. No siree." I struggled, tickling under your arms until you had to let me go. "I'm fat, that's a fact, and we don't need to know the gory details." You spun me around, and I slid you into a waltz, *one* two three, *two* two three, all the way into the bedroom.

*

In the morning, we went out to the garden before breakfast. The sun was rising fast, glaring in our eyes. I crouched down, inspecting the tomatoes, fixing the stakes. "They're ripening, mister. No thanks to you and your piss."

Simon bent down to take a look, shrugging. He toppled me down on my back, crushing a few of the tomato plants along the way, and pushed us into the zucchini. I tried to fight back, but he had my shoulders pinned.

He stood up, facing me, legs on either side of my wide thighs. I knew what he was going to do.

I could have run. I looked up at the sky, at the scorching sun, at his hooded member (do you like that word?) pointed toward my breasts, and I thought, "Run!" (I love that word. Member.) But I wanted to stay.

I tried to angle my chest to catch it. I lay there on my back, the dirt scratching me like bug bites, thinking *pool*. Thinking, my stomach is too convex, bulging with god knows what inside this month, but that space between my breasts is as concave and solid a foundation as ever graced a pool bottom. I can be the template, and you can be what fills it.

But as a swimming pool I was a failure. The piss dripped around the meat of my breasts, trickling onto the ground. Now the whole garden'll be spoiled, poisoned by piss. Poisoned tomatoes, poisoned zucchini, poisoned soil for who knows how long?

I didn't think of it as piss. If I could only hold it in for long enough, it would change color, turn from yellow to swimming pool blue. Like in chemistry, a litmus test. Under the right conditions the fluid would be blue.

Or we could paint it later, give my stomach a good coat of it, until the pool shone as bright and garish a blue as any public swimming pool.

I tried to hold it all in, pushing my breasts together with my hands, making a hand-brassiere. I tried to hold it all in for you. As you sprayed me, I tried to angle my chest just so, so that it would all stay in. But your fingers helped me forget to stay taut, stay tight and ready and solid. Your floor was failing.

*

Uric acid, formaldehyde, chlorine, potato peelings. Later, I looked in my gardening book, but there was no mention of the length of time it would take for the damage to appear. They didn't mention how much piss was necessary to kill a crop, or whether it was animal or human piss or both that was lethal. Piss was listed casually, along with a laundry list of other crop offenders. Urine, formaldehyde, potato peelings, DDT, and chlorine. All common household refuse. All common culprits in crop damage. And here I was, aiding and abetting you.

*

That night, I couldn't sleep. Between the meeting, the episode in the garden, the swimming-pool piss, and Rose's visit, I was worried, a sea of "what ifs" interrupting my hand-thoughts.

What if you're part of their little scheme? What if the Colony closes and I'm left here, alone? What if the Feds really do come for me? What if Rose is right, and my only choice is to go molder away inside a banana kitchen?

So I sat up in the bed, wrapped my robe around me, tying it tight with the sash, and went out into the kitchen, leaving you asleep on top of my covers, curled up in a ball.

On impulse, I put on the orange cloche. Why the hell not? Before I took my seat at the table, I got a glass of cold tap water and fished out half a pack of red licorice I'd hidden behind the red flour jar. A light snack, nothing to disturb the stomach. Max would approve. I cleared off the table, and settled in. Max's voice smoothed away the ifs, the hands, the whys.

Do you remember? he'd always begin. And launch into a hodge-podge monologue about the time Uncle Moe, that alter kocker, was so hot he insisted everyone go naked at the lake but wear blindfolds for modesty, or the time Cousin Gloria lost all her money in canasta at the Party bake-off in the City and had to walk home all the way across the Brooklyn Bridge, walked her shoes right down to the soles of her feet, she did. Max was a good storyteller; I'll give him that. Much better than Sheppie. Now wasn't that a time, I tell you, Max would chortle as he wound up one story, already launching into the next, always one more…

The ringing startled me. At first, I thought it was the phone, but no, I realized in a flash, it was the doorbell.

Did it wake him up? Is he a heavy sleeper? Did they program him to respond to loud noises, like doorbells and gunshots? What if he can't distinguish between them? I hurried to the door.

"Sylvie."

Elaine Schwartz on my doorstep. Ellie Schwartz, ringing my doorbell no doubt to ask me for something. If it wasn't cakes for the Women's Colony Dance, then it was money for the starving German refugees. Such a nudge, that Ellie. How could Joe put up with her all these years? No wonder Wool Cap had left her for Bella.

I stared at her in front of my door. It was morning, I noticed with surprise, early, maybe seven or eight, and already the sun was heating me up.

"I can't bake cakes for any more dances in this heat,

Ellie, if that's what you're here for."

She stared back at me a moment, and gave a barky laugh. A real schnauzer, that woman, with her goddamn committees and bubbemeitzer home cures and coffee cakes. How did Joltin' Joe stand her? "Sylvie, mein Sylvieleh. There won't be any more dances. Didn't you listen to what me and Joe was saying? Did you hear a single word at the last, what, four Mickey Rooneys already?"

"So what brings you here?" I asked, ignoring her rude questions, gesturing her into my kitchen. If Simon appears, I'll tell her he's my nephew, I decided. "Harry."

"We're leaving. Tonight," she whispered in a throaty, loud stage-whisper that could've been picked up by a tape recorder in the basement. She sat down and adjusted her dress, and I flashed on Simon in that same chair in his khakis, surreptitiously moving his privates from thigh to thigh like a paperback book placed awkwardly in his lap.

"Tonight? You and Joe?" I wasn't surprised that she was leaving. Zealots are always the first to jump ship. Just as well.

"You bet. We're going back. To Moscow, Sylvie. Worker's Paradise, the new Colony, 'The Land of the Righteous Proletarians.' Joe's got a contact who's gonna get us on the next ship to Kiev. New passports, new lives, 'working over there to make the Revolution here.'" The Revolution always had a capital *R* when Elaine said it.

"What'll you do with the house?" I knew they hadn't quite finished paying up for it. Which meant the Colony, or whatever the Colony became, would be stuck paying their mortgage. It wasn't like Joe to run off without paying his fair share, but it was just like Elaine.

"Oh, Joe's got that covered. Don't you worry about us," she grinned at me, her yellow front teeth bucking up against her top lip like they were hoping to run away from her tongue.

"Well... that's some news. I'm sure we'll all miss you. Do you need anything?" Please, don't ask for money. I don't want a cent of Max's moolah in that woman's hands.

"Oh no. The Party is taking care of everything. You can go, too, if you want."

"Go? Tonight?" I repeated, unable to imagine myself anywhere but here. I patted my head and felt my cloche. Good, she can remember me in my fancy hat when she's starving her ass off in Bialystok.

"Tonight, next week, whenever. But soon. They're after us, those capitalist pigs, and they'll get us all but good if we don't go soon." They sounded like Joe's words.

"Well, I'll think about it. Thank you." I paused, not knowing what else to say. "You want some coffee?"

Elaine laughed. "I actually came over here because I thought you might want to inherit our coffeemaker. It's the old urn, the one we had back before the Barn was painted." When the Barn was painted. It seemed like a century ago, though it was only six years. It turned into a festival, with busloads of workers coming in from the City just to join in the fun, people coming and going, speakers speaking and everyone eating pound after pound of Elaine's apricot and poppy seed rugelach laid out on Mady's good white linen.

"I don't really need it; I got the one Max's sister gave me." I could still smell that night: Evening of Paris and spit curls, ironed trousers, hard cider, and sweaty kisses. There was an awful play, *Stop those War Drums!* featuring the Colony Youth Players. And then Joe got out his mandolin and everyone danced karubichka, the fox-trot, miserlou at the Lake. At the end of the week, everyone donated something to the Cause: chipped china, an old radio, a giant coffee urn. We were expanding, we were rewiring, we were freshly painted and ready for world revolution. And now we were down to the coffee urn.

"No thanks." Ellie was staring at me like I'd rejected her only son. It's just a coffeemaker, you fool! "But thanks for thinking of me, darling. Leave it at the Barn, and I'm sure we'll find some use for it." I heard Simon cough in the bedroom. I coughed loudly, to cover it up.

"What, you're sick, Sylvie? Everyone's been

worried about you. You've been wandering in and out of the Mickey Rooneys like a golem."

"I'm a little sick, yes. Oy, this weather's getting to me. Heatstroke, you know," I invented, coughing again. I could hear Simon moving, putting on clothes, stretching his arms and legs.

"Can I get you anything? Call Dr. Levitz or run to the drugstore?" she was making little fussing movements with her purse, worrying the latch.

"No, no. I just need to rest. Doctor's orders."

"Then I won't keep you, darling. I just wanted to say good-bye. For me and for Joe. And give you a number to call, in case there's," Elaine lowered her voice back down to a stage-whisper again, "trouble." She fished through her leather monstrosity until she found it: a blue card with red lettering. I took it and scanned it quickly: S. Karnovsky. HQ, L Street Cell. Summerset 8-K79. "Here. That's the magic number if you want to join us...abroad."

"Sure, darling. I'd love to visit you there. If I'm well." I coughed dramatically, bringing up a bit of phlegm.

"Well, I'd better run and pack. Feel better, darling. We'll miss you, Sylvie. Zay gezunt." We hugged and lipsticked each other's cheeks. And she was gone.

Elaine and Joe. I felt a pang of sorrow in my gut, thinking of them leaving. I'll never see those fonfers again. It was a bad sign. When the Party faithful jump ship, the rest are sure to follow. I didn't for a moment believe that they'd make it to Russia; those alter kockers would be buried safe and sound in some suburb in no time, listening to "Midge and Marge," fighting over the gas bill.

I thought of their empty house, the kitchen covered with Party posters printed on paper so thin you could see straight through to the wall. We all had those posters: square-jawed workers in the fields, dressed in overalls, or buxom blondes riding proudly into the sunset on a shiny red tractor. Or a hard hat and his comrades, arm in arm, facing off against a fat, slobbering bossman with a gigantic pimple on his nose. "Workers Unite!" "United We Stand –

Black and White" and "Wages Up—Hours Down, Make New York A Union Town." From *Moscow*, Elaine told us when she'd hand the posters out at meetings, though such slogans made me doubt it.

Now where would they go? When the house was sold to some fine young goyishe banker, a weekend country home, wallpapered over in a cherry print by the wife with only a passing glance, "Look at these ugly old things, honey!"

Or would the Feds take them, catalogue each one as evidence, Exhibit A through Z? "Not enough letters in the alphabet for all those pinko posters," a low-level worker grumbles as he sifts and sorts, tractor blondes in one pile, overalled workers in another. Or would they be discarded, too trivial for trials, and end up decorating your dull gray offices back in Washington, a May Day poster here, a "Free Those Scottsboro Boys" there, a "Workers Unite" stashed beside the water cooler?

I grabbed a pack of half-eaten licorice sticks from the kitchen table and went back to bed. The boy was asleep, curled up kittenish, feet sticking out beneath the sheet.

I should put the boy to work, I thought as I lay down and chewed. It was only right, if he was going to spend so much time lazing around my garden. I'll get him gardening shears, a sun hat, and a pail, and set him to work weeding. Or maybe I'll just have him harvest the zucchini. Yes, that's simpler: just pick them off and pop them in a bag. He'd like that. And then I'd have an excuse, if anyone caught sight of him, shirtless, dirty, digging around in my garden or even guzzling a grape juice in my kitchen.

I took out his satchel from where I'd hidden it in my bedroom closet, and laid it down on the bed beside him. Such a nice satchel. Good wool, silk lining. He could carry his lunch in it while he worked, keep a thermos inside the cool plaid cloth.

He's a local, I'd tell whoever was left to tell, helping me out with the gardening. A good worker, that kid, no trouble. A big help, you know. No trouble at all.

XI. Zucchinis, Folds

"Get up, lazybones!"

No answer.

"If you're spending so much time in my garden, you may as well be gardening. I'll put you in charge of the zucchini. Nu, Simon? That's an easy job if there ever was one. Here, you can harvest them right into this basket."

He groaned. His eyes opened, and he sleepily pulled a lock of hair behind his ear, too long.

Maybe Sylvia could cut it, he thought, twirling it on his finger. Not like Mother, with the stupid yellow bowl and the paper scissors. No, Sylvia's got careful hands; he knows, he's seen her garden. She'll clean up proper, too, no hair left crawling all the hell over the floor. She'll sing as she cuts, one of them Commie songs. Simon hums along: *something, something, Joe Hill last night, alive as he could be.*

Or maybe that's not what you thought. Who knows? All I can say for sure is that you pulled your hair and fell back to sleep.

"Really, Simon, it's so easy. I'll show you how to tug just so, to release them from the vine without hurting the plant."

*

I curled around your sleeping body, spooning you into my stomach, and whispered garden dreams into your ear. "Gardening, Simon. Yes. You'll like it; it's got to be boring just sitting out there all day."

Work is always the answer, we used to say, no matter what the question. I chewed a licorice stick slowly as I whispered. At least Rose thought to bring me a fresh supply of red licorice.

"We could plant some real berries: raspberries, strawberries, wineberries. Sheppie and Gladys have quite a patch of strawberries, so why can't we? Berries and sour cream, specialty of the house. You'll love it. The juice'll spot your hands like a leopard." I tickled where the pink leopard spots would be. "We'll borrow Sheppie's Chevy and drive into the nursery in Lewisboro to buy some starters. Little potted strawberry plants that fit right in the kitchen window. You can help me with the transplant when it's time."

He was fast asleep now, my garden words just another lullaby. I stroked his hands. Good gardening fingers.

*

When I awoke, the clock said 3:30. Night? No, afternoon. An odd hour to wake up to: too early for night, too late to start the day. It was too late to plan your gardening tasks.

I got up and nibbled a bit of red licorice. I'll worry about starting the strawberries tomorrow, I thought as I sank in bed beside you.

My teeth coated in sugar, I counted your fingers instead of sheep. Thumb, forefinger, middle, ring finger, pinkie. You weren't missing any. It would be hard to garden without a full hand. But perhaps they made extras at the factory, a spare thumb for every boy, just in case.

You stayed asleep, but I was wide awake. I wanted to let them know, back at the factory, or wherever the hell, that I knew all about their spying. That I knew you were one of them. I'm no dope; I knew that they planted you there in my garden just so that I would notice poor little Simon, making a mess of my tomatoes, so naked! so vulnerable! so small! and take you into my house. Bastards. I'll show them; I can mess things up, too. I looked at your sleeping face, your delicate features, so sweet, so innocent. Ha! To hell with you, Simon. To hell with all of you.

I got out of bed, went to the kitchen, and pulled out a sheet of paper from the cabinet drawer. It was Eaton 25 lb., 100% linen. The real McCoy: expensive, heavy, fine.

Paper isn't just a passing fancy of mine. Paper airplanes, paper dolls, paper banners, paper babies. Paper factories, paper workers, and of course paper tenements: I've made them all, with only a single sheet. I'm a paper lady.

It's all in the folds. Scissors are for amateurs; a master would never disgrace a page with a cut. Indeed, the whole challenge, the true art of it lies in making an intricate object with the minimum number of creases. I've made a house, complete with balcony, driveway, and shuttered windows, with only four careful folds. Back on Avenue J, I'd outfold Rose every time. I taught her the basics, and a few fancy tricks I can't divulge here, so that she could keep me company on those long rainy autumn afternoons, but she never really got the knack of it.

Our paper was contraband. We stole recklessly from Cousin Lenny's print shop; I'm sure he knew what we were up to, but he never mentioned it. Mama liked to visit Lenny every Tuesday on her day off; she'd drink Russian tea with him, black and scorching hot, sucked through a sugar cube. They'd watch the presses run, catching up on the family gossip, shoptalk, ILGWU rumors. The shop ran the big runs at night; during the afternoon, Lenny would get the type set, then run a test or two, adjusting the ink to make it flow just right. Such a showoff, that Lenny, strutting around his shop puffed up, an adolescent pigeon. Mama loved the presses: "Look, girls, just look at those machines roll!"

Rose and I were less impressed with the presses than the storage closet. We'd climb up the shelves that lined its walls, all the way up to the ceiling. Resting along the way to explore the booty in the boxes, we'd stash ourselves in with the supplies. Rose loved the rulers, regulation army metal gray and shiny, embossed with red numbers. She'd measure everything: the boxes, her bust, my nose. And I'd play along, measuring her waist, lips, the difference in our hands. But it was the paper, stored all the way at the top, reams of twenty-pound white matte paper hugging the ceiling, that I loved.

Crouching high up there, a ream wrapped tight in coarse brown wrapping paper beneath my hand, I felt a weightless excitement. It was like the moment before opening a beautifully wrapped gift when you wonder what is waiting for you. I'd run my fingers lightly over the brown wrapper, and then in one swift move rip it open, and happy birthday, happy birthday to me! a fresh ream would reveal itself to my hand. I'd pull a single sheet ceremoniously—not the top sheet, for that was often damaged, bad luck—and I'd run my hand across it, inhale its bouquet. An image would suggest itself: this one I'll fold into a clown, or a giraffe, no, a flying ace, no no, a baby giraffe: aha, a star! One touch and I knew what this particular piece of paper wanted to be.

The folder's art is an intuitive one; I cannot teach you how to find a giraffe in that piece of paper, that one you're holding, yes, it is meant to be a giraffe, I can feel it. But I can show you.

But not in here. I'll just tell you stories about how I folded, which is the story of how Mama folded:

She'd smile as she'd hold my hand to the paper, talking softly as she pressed just the right amount, there, there, no, there. Paper and Uncle Joe were her prime passions, united in that gold-framed print, the only decoration I remember in our apartment. Stalin at his prime, smiling confidently beneath his furry mustache, ruling over our hallway mirror. A formal pose, hands stiff at his sides, standing in full uniform, painted red and gold. Even Uncle Joe's hair was luxurious, painted a shiny chocolate-brown. I'd stare first at Uncle Joe, then at my own face in the mirror, trying to frown as sternly as Stalin. "Saint Joe. Mama's favorite son," Rose would joke whenever she glanced in the mirror and up at Joe Stalin. Under Saint Stalin we'd fold, me and Mama.

So that's how I got involved with paper. And the Party. (Don't worry; you'll see how this connects to Simon and the story in a moment.) Of the two, I always took paper more seriously. Max was the one who liked to argue about all the details; I was more of a generalist, sure that the revolution was coming soon enough. When I was bored at a meeting, I'd find something to fold. The Party always printed everything on the sheerest, cheapest paper. But it was the thick kind, like in Lenny's shop, that I kept at home, saving it for special occasions, when I wanted to fold lanterns for a party at the Barn, or make paper animals for the children's brigade.

*

So it was a sort of a compliment that I used such an expensive piece of paper on you.

You were still asleep, eyes quiet.

I got up. More licorice? A glass of grape juice? No. I walked into the kitchen.

What now?

My kitchen, my house. One body can't quite own a house. Even with the two of us, the house seemed uninhabited, insubstantial. The objects ready to dance away, the ceiling fan and the coffee cups waltzing out the door, the yellow dishes galloping out the window.

Nothing moved. I left the kitchen to itself, and went back to the bedroom. I pulled the bedroom door shut behind me, feeling it resist. This is the time of year when the house thickens. I went to my desk, feeling the house close around me, and got out the supplies. A page of white linen, Strathmore Pearl, twenty-five pound, the best. Max's best blue fountain pen. Half a pack of red licorice, fresh from Rose's purse. I sat down.

You lay on the bed, asleep. Your fingers were clenched, like a baby who's found a set of keys and won't let go.

The paper cut neatly. Good paper, clean cut.

You bled; it looked like real blood, no movie ketchup for you, but you didn't awaken. A small clean cut; an eighth of an inch, if that.

You didn't flinch. Perhaps you'd turned off, flipped

the switch, shut down for the night. Or maybe you were just tired. Your palm opened, unclenched.

The paper had an inkblot of blood on it, spreading. I dropped the paper and screamed, "Christ!", as if it were my own skin. I ran to the bathroom, slamming doors, pushing the house away. Bandages, cotton swabs, gauze. I grabbed them all, reciting their names in my head: iodine, alcohol, water.

I bandaged you up, and threw away the paper. You stayed asleep.

XII. Red Hots

They've come.

They take me in pieces: a limb from Sheppie, an eye from Gladys, an arm from me. A patchwork girl, our lady of lost limbs, the Colony Lilith.

And then they take me to Washington.

Your Honor, some gray-suited goyishe lawyer declares, look at this monster those stinking commies made. It's like, whaddayacallit, Frankenstein, not even human. They're like insects, these pinkos, Your Honor: no mind of their own. They do whatever Stalin tells them. And look what freaks they've created!

And the arm, *my* arm, wiggles in its foreign socket dying to cry out, "No no, it's you who did this to us. You tore us up! You rearranged us!" But I just flail my foreign arm.

*

I screamed, I flailed, and I woke.

A bad dream, a hot flash.

A golem?

Good morning to all you listeners out there in Radioland, Art Spellman chirped. *It's gonna be another hot one today, so get your fans a-turning.*

"Goddamn this weather!" I yelled, shutting him up with the twist of a button. I didn't remember turning the radio on, but I could damn well turn it off.

In the bathroom, everything hurt. A uterus-full of complaints. I swallowed: a sore, swollen throat full of someone else's morning breath. An aftertaste of bitter lemon. Vomit, sweat, and saliva ran out of my mouth as I didn't make it to the toilet in time.

Even my vomit had a hint of lemon to it. I felt like a toilet, flushed one time too many. When I finally stopped retching I went back into the bedroom, bundled up the soiled sheets, threw them in the hamper, and sat on the stripped-down bed, feeling the heat recede. It's awful to have to clean up your own mess. Where's my Maxie when I need him? Where's my Sheppie-Pie? Bunny needs you, darling. I shivered, thinking of Shep's big warm hands. I was freezing, my fingers green ice.

I looked at the wreck in the mirror: worse.

Yes, since Simon came, it had definitely gotten worse. I poured a cup of tap water and pondered the change in my condition. The change in the Change, Max would've quipped. Mount Sylvia, erupting at odd hours of the night, leaving me coated in my own molten fluids. Flashes? To hell with flashes. These were explosions, not flashes. Even now, half-frozen, I could still feel the heat. Cold sweat poured out of my scalp, my arm pits, my feet. Who knew feet could sweat such rivers? Who knew the Change could last a whole year? I pulled the sheet tighter around me.

Since Simon it was worse. The hot flashes, the vomiting and fuzzy-headedness, the freezing sweat: all worse. Could our...encounters be speeding up the process? Changing the Change?

I cleaned up. It took two showers: one just to scrub it all off, the other to beautify. I sudsed; I shampooed. A bit of Evening of Paris on the wrists, a dab of Pond's under the eyes, and voila! The volcanoes cool, the polar caps melt, the Change calms the hell down.

In the vanity mirror, I took stock. Skin, so much old skin.

I sprayed Evening of Paris in my hair for kicks, fingering the cobalt bottle and the heart-shaped stopper, and walked into the living room, not sure what I was looking for.

In the living room, I surveyed the piles of Max's junk, all that garbage that I hadn't had the heart to throw away. What the hell did he keep in here? Old newspapers, dating back to the twenties. Dusty books, heavy tomes on Marx and Trotsky and bees and plumbing. I walked around the room, inspecting.

I came to Max's desk, a beat-up wooden thing some

Lewisboro schoolmaster must've discarded. The letters. Did he keep the letters? Did I?

I opened the top drawer, and there they were, bundled together with yellow satin ribbons from back when all the girls were wearing yellow. I found the letter I wanted right away. I opened it up, scanned it briefly, and put it back in its blue airmail envelope. Yes, that's the one.

Pocketing it, I marched back into the kitchen, looking forward to reading it again, to hearing Max's voice pine for me in Spain, Simon all but forgotten. Max's letters, ah yes.

I got the coffee perking, wrapped an old shmatte around me, a Rose number, fringed green silk gone threadbare at the elbows, and found my reading glasses beside the phone.

But instead of reading Max's letter, I made up a Simon letter in my head. What would he write about last night? A report, an official report sent to Headquarters:

> Her flesh-coated hand stroked my neck, mouth, cheeks. *Don't wince*, I sternly commanded myself. A jungle of germs sprout in those hands, each caress a carrier. Ugh, so slimy is her touch. Like cow innards rotting in the sun. Or fresh cow dung, or spoilt milk. Something bovine. They love it, don't they: flesh in all its forms. Flesh. Ha! I call it rust.
>
> She turned over, fat stomach on the bed, thick legs flopped to the floor. Jesus, those jelly-roll thighs. Her face turned back to me and she gestured toward her bare pink bottom, smiling. This is marginally better than the hands, I thought.
>
> I took charge: I knew what to do. But then she twisted around, tumbled us so that she was on top, heading south, and I knew what was next. *Don't shoot.* I closed my eyes. *Think of metal.* Clean, freshly shined. *Think of Grandma.* The ugly one with the saggy tits. But it didn't work.
>
> Wet on my cock, wet on my ear, wet on my balls.

> And it was over. I twisted around, pulling myself out of her mouth. Disgusting. It was the moisture that made me yell, ZZZssssss. Oh my poor balls. I rolled off her, and closed my eyes. *Rust.*

Is that what you thought? Is that what you wrote? Possibly. Would you tell them about the incident with the paper?

*

I walked back into the bedroom. He turned over. I watched him cringe, and wondered what he was. Cold angel. Rust robot. Shep son. I lay down, stroking the back of his neck.

"Simple Simon met a pieman."

His face stayed asleep. No groan or twitch of recognition at the stupid lyrics, no response. Nil. I couldn't recall the rest of the words. Louder, with feeling: "SIMPLE Simon MET a pieman."

What comes next?

In the kitchen, I handed him a cup of tea, sweetened with three sugar cubes, no milk. "*Let's* have another cup of coffee, *let's* have another cup of tea," I sang off-key. He dipped his tongue in first, testing, testing, one two three. I made his tea before I perked my coffee, a nicety lost on him, I'm sure.

"*Let's* have another cup of tea." I couldn't stop singing, even though I could tell it was annoying him. He wiped his mouth on his napkin, and glared at me with those cold Sheppie eyes. Old eyes.

"Okay, enough of that. You don't have to drink it if you don't want to." I took his hand and kissed it. It froze under my lips, dead hand, drowned fingers. My lips had done whatever the opposite is of breathing life into someone.

Did they cut the juice? Or did my kiss do it? Did this extra heat I'm generating courtesy of the Change sizzle from my lips to his lips, burn through the fine silt of his skin, short-circuiting the mess of wires that lay beneath the deceptively fleshy surface?

Or was he dead?

Just a runaway teenage hoodlum, a Lewisboro local, dead in my bed? That will look real nice in the papers, Sylvie. Maybe it was the paper cut that did it: infection. A rare blood disease. Death.

Just as I was about to panic, Simon opened his eyes wide and giggled.

"Real funny, mister, playing dead like that. Give me a kiss, lazy bones, and maybe I'll forgive you and make us a nice breakfast." I pulled him to me by his dog-tag chain and he kissed my neck, or planted something.

It didn't feel like a kiss. I felt something growing there. A new sex organ, unfamiliar in feel, sprouting on my neck for you, hard and red as an erection, but soft against your lips. I stood still, feeling it grow.

I didn't move. I lay still, my arms wrapped around you, as you pressed or planted or something-elsed my neck. I pulled your long weedy body on top of mine.

I didn't do anything back to you. Neck, neck, neck... whatever was happening there swallowed me in neck. After a minute I felt I should do something, anything, to acknowledge you, so I patted your back in gentle small strokes. I licked your cheek. It was sweet, not salty, with a faint undertone of lemon. You were completely on top now, groaning as you rubbed hard against me, teeth fastening into my neck. I pulled your head from my neck to mouth and forced my tongue in, finding nothing planted there. Except that sound.

"ZZZZsssss," I hissed back.

*

It was much later. Dinnertime. I looked out: zucchini and more zucchini. I thought of Rose, always hoarding her vegetables like other kids hoarded candy.

The phone rang. "Sylvie. Gladys."

"I can't talk now, darling. I gotta go make some dinner. For Harry," I explained, as though she cared.

"Yes. Well there's an emergency meeting. You gotta come, tomorrow. To our place. It's serious goldenrod, Sylvie. The Nebraska isn't even the half of it. Nobody's safe."

"All right, all right."

"We're Mickey Rooneying at my place; we think the Barn is bugged, um, Nebraska-ed. You gotta come. Tomorrow, ten sharp..."

*

The garden was a mess. Everything was going to zucchini; the lettuce, beans, and carrots all crowded out. Even the radishes were having a hard time. I saw footprints, broken stalks, crop damage. He'd been messing around in my garden again.

At least most of the tomatoes held their own, safely rooted and staked. A perfect German Johnson with salt, the only heirloom tomato that has as much flavor as a mutt, according to the sages at Burpee: oh yes, that's what we'll have. I looked more closely; no, the Germans were still green, only slightly mottled with orange. It would have to be zucchini.

No; I want spinach. Canned creamed spinach, I thought wickedly. To hell with zucchini. I opened a can from the pantry and threw the lumpy mass into a pan.

Simon ran past me, knowing how to slide the glass doors open now in one smooth move, and headed straight to the bathroom, shutting the door behind him.

I followed, standing behind the closed door, waiting. I heard the water running in there, and the flush of the toilet. It ran and ran. I scurried back into the kitchen, not wanting him to catch me listening.

I stood at the glass door, looking out. Some of the tomato plants were still toppled, but most had been repaired. How sweet of him, them, whoever. I heard the toilet flush, and sniffed the air. Smoke?

I sniffed again. Yes, something was burning. Smoke filled the hallway. I walked to the bathroom door, still closed. He's probably short-circuiting, water hitting live wires as he tries to wash his hands.

What should I do?

What could I do? I panicked. I couldn't let him burn up. I couldn't let him burn my house up, either.

I retreated into the bedroom. It smelled like burned rubber. I leaned back onto my carefully made bed, drinking it in, liking its stink. Smoke kills more frequently than fire, I recalled from some workers' safety film. If you smell smoke, don't wait for flame: run. Run!

Just as I was getting up to make my escape, it hit me: the spinach.

"Goddamn spinach!" I said the words aloud, laughing with relief, plunking my ass back down on the bed. It wasn't the boy who was burning; it was just the goddamn spinach cooking itself to death on my goddamn stove.

I raced back into the kitchen, turned off the flame, dug the burned spinach out of the bottom of the pot with a fork and flicked it into the garbage, opened the glass door to let in some fresh air, and ran back into the bedroom, giggly and quick, like a kid playing tag. But he'd beat me to it. With a white towel tied around his waist, he stood in my doorway.

"Are you hurt?"

"Ssszzz, sszzzz, ssszzzz." It was softer now, but persistent, like a refrigerator trying to keep things cool on a hot day.

I inspected. He seemed okay. His eyes looked better, the pink swamp clearing back to white. And he was clean. And we were stepping up onto the bed. Not in, but on, hurrah.

I took off the towel, forgetting all about the smoke and spinach. His thing dangled between us. We were both eyeing it.

It jerked up and down, as if to nod in agreement:

yes, yes. My hand wanted to hold it, but instead, took the towel and twisted it around his head, turban-style. Small balls, hung low for a boy. His blue eyes brightened as his thing kept bobbing in assent, yes, Sylvie, yes.

"The Sheik of Araby," I proclaimed, and he laughed. It was a throaty laugh, too deep and gritty for such a small clean boy. "Kiss me, you silly sheik you," I said in Max's joking intonation, and my hand found its way down to him.

He pressed down my breasts with his palms, holding them rigid and flat. What perfect white teeth, lined up like soldiers, ready for combat. I swallowed his mouth up in mine, my thick lips covering his, kiss, kiss, oh darling... I stopped.

I grabbed his dog tag, pirated the tag into my mouth, tasted the inscription, *Simon,* cursive. I spat it out, and opened his lips with my fingers, pressing my pointers down his throat for bugs, plants, radios. His teeth bit down hard on my fingers and sucked. Groaning, I tried to pull them out, but he bit harder.

He clasped my breasts tighter and we jumped. Bounce, bouncy, bounce: trampoline-style, gaining height, we jumped on my bed. My fingers dug deeper with each bounce, bounce, bounce.

And all fall down. He wrestled me for the top and everything went to fadeout. Not blackout, but a slow fade, the primary colors draining away from the room one at a time, leaving a wash of gray as his clean face loomed over mine.

Is this how fainting feels? I thought, still smelling spinach. I'd never fainted before. Or is he drugging me?

And then, a split second before I was completely out, I heard the boy say, "Sylvia?" in a mannish voice from nowhere.

XIII. Flash

You can only see the hornworms at night. By day, they blend into the greenery, their scaly heads invisible against the green leaves of the tomato plants. But at night they glow. Yellow, not white, no Vegas razzle-dazzle. To the naked eye, their weak light is barely visible, easily overlooked as your gaze flickers across the garden.

But I know how to see the hornworms glow. I take Max's old army flashlight, rig it up with an ultraviolet black bulb I order special from Harold's Army Navy on Fourteenth Street in the Village, and then out I go.

Under the flashlight, they glow a soft bluish white. If you weren't looking for it, you'd miss it. They look like broken bolts of lightning, wiggling on the leaves, groups of them, one-inch long a piece, gnawing on my plants. I glow, too, when I put on Max's dirty white fishing cap, and my white lace house dress, and my white tennis shoes, hold the flashlight at arm's length and point it back at me. Do the hornworms see me glow? I don't know how they see colors, or if they can even perceive light and dark. They certainly see my tomato plants, though. Maybe they see only tomatoes, their whole universe a spectrum of green and red. Or maybe it's the smell that draws them. A hornworm blindly wiggles its nose to catch the bitter perfume. Yes, I think I've read of that.

I use Max's fishing hat to knock them off the plants, one at a time. I can't bring myself to touch them. A few whacks with the hat and they're flying onto the ground. Stamp, squash, and so long, tomatoes. Another hornworm exits this world. Off to worm hell or heaven.

*

That night, after the spinach incident, I woke up alone, long before dawn, with only one thought: hornworms. I've been neglecting the goddamn hornworms. I got into my getup, grabbed the flashlight and Simon's satchel, the red plaid number I'd stashed in my bedroom closet. I went out to the garden, sniffing the air, trying to think like a hornworm.

But instead of hornworms, I found Simon. He'd curled up beneath a large stake with three tomatoes dangling above him. In the dark, the tomatoes looked like giant grapes.

His mouth hung open. I could see the pink tip of his tongue, lolling between his teeth. He lay on his side, his hands folded between his knees. Even lying down, he had that cocky slump.

I shined my fluorescent straight on him until he let out a small growl. I kneeled down. The ground was cool, fresher than the air.

"What are you? " I asked in a loud, boisterous voice, aiming the tunnel of light at his eyes. Startle him into speech: surprise the words out of him, let the light shine him straight into a complete conversation, a word, a groan, a "wha?" Anything. If you can say my name, you can damn well speak. Speak already, goddamn you! Pretty please?

He grabbed the satchel from me and put it under his head like a pillow. And that's the last I saw of it. Maybe it's still buried in the garden somewhere, or maybe it's in your office with Ellie and Joe's old propaganda posters. Exhibit S.

"Come on, Simon. It's too cold to sleep out here tonight." It wasn't cold; I don't know why I said that.

"Urgh?" A grunt, a cough, and then only a bleary stare. No words. Silence, except for the crickets, singing their tuneless chants. I shined my flashlight right in his eyes.

Dirty whore! Hameshe Kurve! Class traitor! My head flooded with voices. They know my weaknesses, my voices do. Fat dried-up old sow! Exploiting the workers! Exploiting the youth! Where's your solidarity with the proletariat? Class traitor! Shtupping the enemy, eh? And on Max's sheets, no less. Stupid old ninny. Your political immaturity is clear. You're a turncoat, a double agent. You never were anything more than a fellow traveler, anyway.

It was bad enough when you were kanoodling with Comrade Sheppie. But this is it. We'll take your party card away for that, you stupid bitch.

Traitor. Turncoat. Slut. I kissed him, traitor, slut, kurve, a curse for each kiss, oh yes.

*

In the morning, my nipples woke me up. His fingers were busy, pinching too hard. "Ouch!" I yelled groggily, batting him away. Undeterred, he replaced his fingers with an eager mouth, rolling his slender hips on top of mine.

Breasts he knew. Some tastes your tongue never forgets. When you grow gummy again, Simon my friend, sixty-odd years from now, your tongue will still recall that taste. That special bosomy flavor. That you tried to suck out of me that morning, suck away thirteen years of pizzas and milk shakes.

I pushed him off me, "Suck yourself, Simon," and put his pinky finger into his own mouth. He lay on his back, compliant, and sucked.

Something hurt. I inspected my breasts carefully.

There were marks. Not just the usual surface wounds that lovemaking leaves on fair-skinned redheads, but distinct and deep tooth marks. Two of them, an inch apart, a quarter-inch above my left nipple.

"Look what you've done, you naughty boy," I scolded, rolling toward him. "Naughty, naughty Simon."

Deftly I pulled his pinky out of his mouth, and touched the cause: incisors, twin perpetrators glinting white. Simon the Sucker. Simon the Biter. Simon the Wounder. He bit down on my hand, too hard.

I slapped your face with my free hand, "Bad Simon."

The shock of the slap unclenched your jaws. I pulled out my hand, and leaned back in the bed. But I kept slapping your face, harder. My face close to your face, so close I could smell you on my fingers, lemon cleanser mixed with ordinary morning breath.

"Finger me."

I lay back in my bed and closed my eyes stroking the tooth marks above the nipple, repeating my command, "Finger me." One finger found its way; the rest soon followed. Did they train the boys in the nitty-gritty, give them a special course in a schoolroom somewhere deep inside the old factory on advanced lovemaking?

"Deeper." I liked manning the ship, the boy standing ready at the controls.

But he disobeyed.

*

Your hand remembers what happened. Your fingers have perfect recall. Oh yes they do. Let me refresh each finger:

I felt it go in.

The device was inserted; that's all I'll say. I couldn't see it, but I felt it, all right. Metallic. Small. Listening.

XIV. Dirt

"Out!"

Don't you touch him, you've already done enough harm, I scowled silently to myself. Get him out, wash yourself up, fish the device out, and get to the meeting. Come on, Sylvie old girl, leave well enough alone, you dirty old bitch. Don't touch him again. Not once more.

But I couldn't help it; I was shaking his shoulders awake. "Out, Simon! Get the hell out of here. I need to get to my meeting."

He squinted at me, cockeyed. One hand waved out toward me, gesturing. Indicating what?

He did it again, a flick with the hand, ending with a point toward the door this time. What the?...

It was me. He was mimicking me, the little shtunk.

That was it. "It's not funny, mister. Goddamn you, GET OUT!!" I screwed up my face, trying not to think of his face screwing up in response.

But he didn't mimic. He got out of bed and stood up, right in front of me, facing me. On his feet, he looked older. Sixteen, maybe seventeen. He scratched his stomach, lips twisting into a casual sneer. Coarse dark hair furred his cheeks, underarms, crotch, but underneath, the skin was still soft.

He bolted. I don't know how he found his way out the kitchen door; there are three glass panels, a triptych, and only the least likely one on the far right has a latch that opens. If it were me, I would have guessed the one on the left, but he knew it was the right.

I sat in the middle of the bed, my breasts drooping heavy and sore. If I could scream, everything would be fine.

I'd open my mouth wide, and let a perfect cry sing out, carrying with it all the fat and heat and terror clogging me up. So I let out a shout, opening my jaw as far as I could.

"AAAH!"

But it was only a short, quick grunt, and my breasts still ached and I was confused and *help me, Max, Mama, even*

Rose goddamn her, yes, even her, help me, help, oh christ goddamnit help me!

In the bathroom, I drank water until the choking stopped, brushed my teeth twice, ran a comb through my hair, and avoided the mirror. Bending over, I tried to fish the thing, the device, out, but it was gone. Gone, I tell you! Who knows how? It dissolved or fell out or was pushed deeper in. For all I know, it's still in there, rusting away.

I noticed the toilet seat was up. Without thinking, I grabbed a tissue and pressed it against the back side of the toilet seat. At least I've got his fingerprints, I thought as I put them in the top drawer of my dresser with the others I'd been collecting off of cups, glasses, the bandanna, and even the tomatoes. That's some consolation. They can bug me, but I can bug right back. Or at least collect evidence.

Evidence. I liked that word. My spirits lifted.

"It's meeting time, meeting time, it's time for meeting time," I sang in a cheery, folk-songy voice.

I threw on a blue housedress, grabbed my purse from the kitchen, pulled out a red licorice stick and chomped it down, and ran out the front door, not checking to see if he was back in my garden.

"It's meeting time, meeting time, it's time for meeting time."

Out of habit, I started down Old Colony Road, tripping on the pebbles scattered in the shoulder. Unpaved roads: one of the most distinctive and annoying features of our Colony. Other colonies gave in after the War, but we stayed unpaved. "We're untarred, unfeathered," Mady Feld would chirp whenever some skinny boychik, fresh out of City College, would earnestly suggest, as though no one had ever thought of it, that for the Collective Good, we pave the roads.

I stared at my feet walking, doubting the goddamned dirt. What was the point of all our stupid squabbles over tar, dirt, slate? Tomorrow they might come and pave the streets with gold, just like our parents had expected back in the shtetls of Lvov. Pave right over our dead bodies, yeah, I can see it now: shoot first and pave later, in a fake gold stone laid down by non-union Negroes.

Or maybe we'll finally do the job ourselves. Anything to show old Joe McCarthy and his lot what a swell, patriotic bunch we are. We'll be Levittowned, duplexes popping out from under the old oak trees, in-ground pools and popsicles overrunning the Barn, the Lake, infecting the whole goddamn Colony like goldenrod. The Barn will be just another town hall for tax collectors and traffic cops to waste the day inside. Perhaps people will wonder why they didn't build a brick Colonial for the purpose, muse over how a musty red barn came to be a state building. Or, more likely, no one will wonder at all.

Or, most likely, they will tear it all down, replace the dark red wood and beamed awnings with the requisite brick and brass. I've been to New Jersey. I've seen those old-fashioned Colonials rise up overnight. As I stopped in front of the Barn, I looked up at the roof and imagined its high, slanted wood ceiling straightening into a brick square.

XV. Ducks

No one was inside. I tried to remember something Gladys had said on the phone: emergency meeting, the Party was trying to take our houses back, I had to come, Ellie and Joe had already left, such a scandal it was...now what was it? Oh yes – "Better to Mickey Rooney at somebody's house?" she'd stage-whispered in a questioning tone of voice, as though the bugs could only pick up loud, declarative statements, "so it looks more like a, whaddayacallit, a ladies coffee klatch? Come to our place at ten, but don't ring the bell. We'll leave the back door unlocked. The lights will be off, and we'll all be down in the basement."

And I'd forgotten. Am I going senile already? Oy gevalt. Now I was late, and I'd have to walk all the way up Danger Road to Gladys and Sheppie's in my pink heels.

Take my house, my ass, I thought as I made my way up Danger Road. These Party fonfers think they can steal the ship, even as the Feds are sinking it? Nuts to them. I stubbed my toe, cursing the Party, cursing Danger Road. What a name. Not too subtle, eh Simon? It curved straight up the hill behind the Barn. Gladys and Shep were the only ones who built up there: "Because we love 'danger,'" Gladys always joked. They had to park their Chevy down at the Barn, though; no car could handle the crazy-cat incline of Danger Road.

As I walked by their car, I knocked the windshield, just in case. A boy could hide out in a car like this. He could snuggle up in the bucket seats, sleep safe and sound each night between the wood-paneled sides of the Chevy. No one goes anywhere at night in the Colony; surely he'd figured that out by now. He wasn't stupid; just quiet. He noticed things. Not just the obvious things, either, but stuff no human would ever notice. A roomful of bleeping machines shrunk down to the head of a pin, lodged inside his head, buried but ticking, working, recording every detail of every goddamn tree, every leaf, mouth, tit as it hits his brain.

Am I right?

Still you won't tell me. Why not? It can hardly matter now, can it? Eh?

*

Anyway, my ankle gave a little as I hiked up Danger Road. There are stories about this hill. It was an Indian burial ground, some say, a place too obscure for even the most restless of dead souls to escape. No, no, the locals said; Danger Road was a warpath, used by the Iroquois to lay siege to the settlers sleeping unawares down in Lewisboro a century back! But Louie says, and I'm inclined to believe him, that it has nothing to do with the Indians; it's just called Danger Road because it's so steep and dark. The first Colony folks, Joe and Elaine, Bella and Wool Cap, we named it that, he said. The ones who started it all, trekking out from Brooklyn on the weekends, their faces work-weary, surprised and scared and thrilled by all this wilderness. Danger Road cuts straight up Danger Mountain, running through a dense stand of fir trees. And then it dead ends, in front of the ramshackle split-level Sheppie built with his own two hands. He loved to say that: "With my own *two* hands," as if he might have had three.

As I walked up the driveway to Shep and Gladys', it was too still, like even the wind had been assassinated. Too quiet. All the lights were off in the house. The driveway, true to form, was unpaved, filled up with small white stones. Better to be a stone right now.

A woman's laugh broke the silence. The laughter doubled: no, it was two women. I stopped, staring at all the stones in the driveway, thinking of how much work it must've taken Shep and the boys to quarry, ship, and place them there.

I believe in work. Yes, I do. In workers. And in stone. And slabs of meat, marbled with fat, hanging in a line at the butcher's. Yesiree. And Revolution. Revolution Now! Like we used to yell at the shop canteen at lunch time to cheer ourselves up. Some liked to sing the "Internationale" because it bugged Mr. Lewin, the line boss, but I just liked to yell.

So I yelled, anything to break the silence, as I made my way up the driveway, the white pebbles tripping me as I walked. "Revolution *Now*! Revolution *Then*! Revolution *Forever*!" The laughter inside had stopped.

I stumbled up to the front door and let myself in. It was Colony policy: we all shared a skeleton key. The house was full. Long faces lined the kitchen table.

"Hello Sylvia. 'Lo, Sylvie. Heya. Hi, stranger."

"Okay, she's here. So let's start already," Mady barked, adjusting her purple scarf tighter around her shoulders, despite the heat.

"Comrades, Workers: We got four items on the agenda: first, and I guess foremost, is Louie's move from last meeting to return the Barn to the Party. Following that, we gotta vote on how we divvy everything else up, homes included, and title the land. Then we gotta talk bugs, surveillance, spies, and how to keep them from nailing us. And what's that last thing? Oh yes, Shep and Gladys have brought us some delicious raspberries which I will divide equally to all comrades present." She paused, glaring at everybody. "And for the record, as you probably all know already, Elaine and Joe flew the coop."

"The damn sneaks! Ellie didn't even call me..." Gladys started it, but the hurricane of rage was bigger than even her mouth. It galed, gaining force as it stormed through the room. *They said they were going to Moscow. Can you believe it? Moscow my ass; Joe told me personally they were heading for Tenafly. Joe in Jersey! Can you believe it? That chalushisdicht bastard! Class traitors! Turncoats!*

"On to item number one, comrades!" Mady shouted, pounding her cane.

But she couldn't thump them back to her agenda. The conversation moved from the awful subject back to objects. *Who gets the electric washing machine from the Barn's basement? Who gets the collective coffee table?* So much sunken treasure!

And other, whispered conversations began: *I'm going to Scarsdale, my cousin's got a real cheap property out there ready and waiting. I got a job out in Queens, an auto shop. You want for me to see if I can get you something? I got a friend who said we can stay with him in Yonkers until we get back on our feet. I know a real estate guy, Eddie Finsky, yeah, that guy, he's a real mensch, trust me, he's my Cousin Izzie's wife's brother, who can sell off the whole Colony in one fell swoop. No kiddin'.*

"Let's discuss item four: comrades, who wants raspberries?" Mady was determined to at least accomplish the equitable division of berries. Shep smiled his blank smile, eyes looking like he'd already left for greener pastures. I remembered that look.

It's tomato time, I decided. These fine fonfers are worrying about pliers and coffee tables; I got a garden waiting for me. In one breath they talk about giving the Barn back to the Party, and in the next it's back to berries. Why should I bother with them anymore? I'll do what I want, without any more proposals or votes or meetings. Let the Party take the Barn; fine. I got the deed to my house, and they'll have to steal me to steal it. And I'm not leaving. Colony or no Colony, I'm staying.

That's right, I'm not leaving. They gotta come take me by force, kicking and screaming. Rose can't make me leave, and these jokers can't, either. Max would laugh at these old Colony hacks, going on with their goddamn meetings even as the Feds close in. What a bunch of alter cockers. Don't listen to them, Sylvie. Be true to the cause. Listen to Maxie. Listen to your garden.

I slipped out between a vote on the fate of the tea kettle and a discussion of recent Nebraska incidents. No more meetings, I swore to myself as I stumbled down the white-stone driveway, a pebble caught in the toe of my shoe. Some will stay, some will go, but I'm not listening to any more of this bubkes. Ganug. Enough, darling.

*

I didn't notice you in the garden. I was still thinking about the meeting, shaking my head with annoyance. I made some coffee, pulled out a lone, dusty licorice stick from my apron, and chomped furiously. Goddamn them all. I'm not leaving, and I'm not wasting any more of my time on them. Not on Sheppie, either. To hell with him. I folded the wrapper into a bear.

Rap, rap. The noise startled me out of my silent rant.

Simon was knocking, fists pummeling the sliding-glass door. That's an odd noise, isn't it, fists on glass? He did it continuously, rap rap rap, using both fists. I walked over to him, faced him squarely, only the glass between us, but he kept right on rapping. I thought of rapping back, mirroring his fists with mine.

He looked sick.

"Do you want to come in?" I barked. "'Cause if you do, you have to ask." The dog tag glinted in the late-afternoon sun, a metal insect pollinating his chest.

He glared at me. He still had that stupid red bandanna around his neck. Otherwise, he was naked, sunburned, dirty. His nose was running.

"You have to ask, Simon. Nicely," my voice flirted, in spite of my annoyance.

He smiled. With his index finger, he smeared the words backward on the glass: *Can I com in*? No *e*.

XVI. Waking, Talking

Days passed. I don't recall how many. Some days you came, some days you didn't.

Eventually, it was July. We heard rockets shooting on the 4th, kids from Lewisboro whooping and cheering as the firecrackers hit the sky, opened quick like morning glories, and vanished. We listened, but we didn't venture out to watch the show.

But most of the time, there was silence when you came, and silence when you didn't come.

Days and nights and days and days passed. No one else came. And I never left. We made do with the food left in the pantry, mixing the canned goods with the zucchini from the garden. I found a stash of red licorice in the basement I'd hidden from myself when I'd gone on a reducing diet years ago. They were a bit tough, but we liked them anyway. We chewed slowly, making it last, our lips and tongues magenta, lying in bed, or on the sofa, or at the kitchen table. But no one came. No more meetings, and no more talk of leaving. Maybe most of them were already gone. We didn't care.

We had our routine. Most of it's a blur now, the way days that repeat themselves tend to blur. I do recall one particular day. You'll see why:

We woke up drenched in sweat. It was hotter than ever. It had rained the night before, but instead of clearing the air, it just made it more humid.

I fed him, bathed him, bathed myself. We walked into the living room with nothing but blue towels around our waists.

I gave him a drink, grape juice, most likely, and asked him about school, fishing, the rainstorm last night. He just listened, silent.

"I know, I'll teach you French. Would you like that?"

Simon made a face.

"Well, I don't know French, but I could learn it, and teach you. French, the international language of diplomacy. You could be a diplomat, Simon."

Another face.

"Okay, if you don't like French, how about Esperanto? 'The Tongue of Tomorrow.' It's easier than French, I hear."

He rolled over, away from me.

"We can go away. Somewhere safe. We'll go to Russia, wear fur hats and babushkas, eat borscht with all the other workers. Everything will be equal, not a farblongdet mess like here. I'll grow tomatoes in the town's collective garden. I'll be famous for them."

Simon rolled back, kissed my cheek, and closed his eyes.

I kept talking, drifting from Russia and tomatoes back to the meetings, the Barn, Rose, and back again to the tomatoes.

Stop dancing those old skeletons, Max would say when I'd brood about the old times. Live in the present, Sylvie. He hated my remember whens: when milk cost a nickel, when we rubbed against each other at that rally in Union Square, when we danced out by the Lake that first summer, naked, alone. "Yeah yeah," Max would grouse. "Enough already. Leave the past dead and buried, where it belongs. Didn't your mother ever tell you to leave well enough alone?"

My mother left nothing alone. She was a toucher, grabbing my arm and squeezing it and whispering too close to my ear in that loud smoky stage whisper that, sad to say, Rose has inherited: "Sylvie. Darling. Did I ever tell you about the time Uncle Sid ate a raw codfish? The whole thing, he did. That's how hungry he was, seven days without a meal he went." With Mama, everything was given the same importance. Remember when Sid ate that codfish? Remember when we found out Cousin Charlie was a turncoat? You're too young to remember the time Aunt Sylvie-who-you're-named-for rode a horse without a stitch of clothing on her. You remember, of course, that Cousin Sammy raped a peasant girl.

What Mama most enjoyed remembering was who wore what, twenty-five-or-more years ago, down to each ribbon and stocking. Not that she had grand clothes; not that any of them—cousins, mothers, brothers, neighbors—had more than one good outfit. But oh how she loved the details of dresses worn, dresses sewn, dresses coveted. Your first birthday, you wore that pink taffeta and the white kneesocks with the lace trim, with the matching pink bows in your hair. Oy how you hated me braiding your hair! When little Sol died, I sat shiva in that black shmatte with the long train and mutton sleeves; we didn't have money for a new one. And years later, Rose sewed pearl buttons down the front, and wore it for her graduation, looking like a movie star! A sheine maidel she was, in that dress. You probably don't remember the dress you wore to Papa's funeral. You were only three; how could you? Beautiful china blue silk it was. And that blue silk pinafore with the white piping Rosie sewed for you? She made it from the very same bolt of cloth, ten years later! Do you remember? Mama would squeeze my hand, excited by the overstuffed closet of dresses in her head. What would she have made of this boy, with so few clothes to remember? A dirty red bandanna. Khaki pants, bagging at the waist. A peach undershirt.

That peach—it reminded me of something. Peekskill!

"Do you want to know about Peekskill? The real story, not the one you read in the paper? I'll give you the skinny on Peekskill. Maybe it will solve a few things."

Simon had fallen asleep on the couch, somewhere between the story of Mama's dresses and my Party membership. I didn't care; I knew something was listening. I could hear it, clicking and whirring as he slept.

"Hey, sleepyhead Simon," I repeated. He blinked, and didn't protest being awakened. "Do you want to know about Peekskill? The real story, not the garbage you read in the paper." He yawned. "I'll tell you the dope about Peekskill. Maybe it will solve a few things."

XVII. Peekskill, Eyeballs

I got stuck making the salami sandwiches. Sandwiches! A pisher of a job. A girl's job. Not a job for a Women's Action Committee Leader. Yes, I was a leader back then, Simon, believe it or not. And I was furious to be stuck with sandwiches. Corn beef on rye, pastrami on rye, salami on rye. A schmear of mustard and a sour pickle and some chips. My hands stank with sandwiches all through the drive to Peekskill. There's something deathly about that cold-cut smell under the nails.

"Don't forget the mustard, Sylvie," some alter kocker called to me as I sat at the table in the Barn with my meat laid out. I ignored him.

"There you go, boychick, happy trails," I joked as I plopped the sandwich bags into a line of cardboard boxes. Lots of sandwiches, for lots of comrades. Who knew how many?

As I finished packing up the sandwiches, I forgot my annoyance. It wasn't just us going to Peekskill to hear Paul Robeson, but all the other colonies dotting the area: Followers of the Trail, Camp Kinderland—they'd all be there. And a busload or two of folks from the City, too! It was Labor Day, so all the workers were momentarily freed from the gray factory floors, happy to get on the bus, out to the country for a day of solidarity and sandwiches. Solidarity in Peekskill! Solidarity in Westchester! Sandwiches for the masses!

We piled onto yellow school buses someone had borrowed for the day. Hillsdale Elementary, the buses declared in green block letters painted on the sides. It was a short drive; Peekskill is close, only twenty minutes west of Sylvan Lake, but I remember it as clear as Mama remembered crossing from Russia.

"Sit with me, Bunny," Sheppie gestured to the seat beside his, the window seat, his hand fluttering across it with a girlish gesture. The seats were kid seats, low-backed green plastic, too narrow for our grown-up asses.

I sat beside Shep but didn't say a word, looking out the window as we pulled out of the Barn, down Old Colony Road. Max wasn't going on this trip, so I figured it was okay to sit with Sheppie. "Have yourself a time, Sylvie," Max had said that morning before I left the house, sarcasm edging his words. "Be a good girl." He pet my hair and kissed my hand before I walked out the door, as if to put his mark on me. Max didn't go anywhere much that year, just grumped around the Colony, fixing one thing, only to break another. It was 1945, the year Max was getting sick. But we didn't know it then; we thought he was just getting cranky.

I was pretty cranky myself that afternoon, ignoring the rounds of "If I had a Hammer" and Sheppie's wry little comments about the bourgeois bus driver's plaid pants as the bus drove through the countryside. We knew there could be trouble. The papers blared "Negro Red to Raise the Rabble in Peekskill!" I'd heard, just that morning on 94.3 FM, on the supposedly liberal "News and Views" hour with Art Spellman, a warning that the Commies and Negroes were invading Peekskill. Such garbage, on "News and Views," no less!

Sheppie was talking, the others were singing in rounds, but I just looked out the window. Fall was coming on. I watched the yellow-tinged trees rush by, thinking about the day to come. Workers, locals, Paul Robeson, lunch meat: oy veh. I ran my fingers through my hair. My hands still smelled of salami.

The picket signs left over from the last May Day march on Union Square were propped up in the front seats like eager schoolchildren, their shiny white faces proclaiming "Justice Now!" and that long, awkward Thomas Paine quote the boys in the Lincoln Brigade were so fond of: "We fight not to enslave, but to set a country free, and to make room upon earth for the honest men to live." The old picket signs and seltzer filled the bus; someone had heard that there'd be no water at the concert, so we piled box upon box of seltzer, extra seltzer, vanilla, cherry, and egg-cream seltzer, just in case. And those damn salami sandwiches.

I was still annoyed, unable to catch the enthusiasm for the protest that was inflaming everyone else.

"Sylvie-Bunny, give a little smile for your old Sheppie-pie. Come on Bunny, don't be funny, kiss your funny," Shep grinned, squeezing my hand.

So he's rhyming now. What will he think of next? I ignored him, and stared out the window, trying to lose myself in the colors of the trees.

*

Cops and beer. That was Peekskill that night: blue cops everywhere, smacking their billy clubs in their palms. Peekskill wasn't much in those days: a few shops, a bar, a post office, and a bunch of farms. But it was crawling with cops that night. Too many cops to be locals; they must have called in the State boys.

And beer: kegs full, opened helter-skelter, the local yokels liquored up and dripping foam, peering out at us from storefronts and Chevrolets like a bunch of overfed roosters.

"Be careful, Bun," Sheppie whispered in my ear as I stepped off the bus onto Peekskill. Of what?

The concert was just grand. We sang along with Paul; we chanted with Paul; we were as noble and strong and brilliant as Paul.

"Paul! Paul! Paul!" the women cried. "Solidarity Now! Solidarity Forever! Solidarity with the Negroes, the workers, the downtrodden of the world!"

Swing low, sweet chariooooot. He sang, he spoke, he charmed, his deep river voice traveling the night, no microphone needed. My brothers, my sisters, we unite for justice. He moved from song to speech to chant without missing a beat. "Justice! Peace! Unity!" the men and women and Paul cried. We unite for peace. We unite for the International Struggle for workers' freedom. I stand with you here, my comrades, together in struggle. Sing with me!

Sing together with all your brothers and sisters! I grew hoarse, singing and chanting along, caught up for once in the glory of the moment.

The advance word had been right: no water. Swing low, sweet dry chariot. So we put up a stand giving out free seltzer in yellow Dixie cups left over from the school bus. Old man river, swing low. Pure joy, such joy, spread wide as Paul's smile over the crowd as we passed out the cups and kept on singing, chanting, uniting. Sure, the coppers and the townies stood frowning a circle around us, but we didn't care. Peace! Now! Freedom! Now! Coming for to carry me home. Towards the end, as Paul sang "Swing loooow, sweet chariooooot" for one last time and the crowd roared, Sheppie swept me up, bride-over-the-threshold-style, and kissed me hard. My mouth loved it, ate it, peace now, freedom now, swing low now, kiss me now, oh now, sweet chariot, now –

"Fucking nigger-loving kikes!"

The voice echoed in the dry night sky. We were a big group, a few hundred strong, but packed tight in Peekskill Park around the podium, we could all hear that nasty, loud woman's voice. She repeated it, "Fucking nigger-loving kikes! Go back where you come from, you dirty pinko Yids!"

Other voices followed, but that was first.

Second: the cops. Orange-cheeked, brandishing their flashlights in our face, like rabid pumpkins they circled us. Some joined in the name-calling, some waved their billy clubs and gestured at the guns stuffed in their pants legs. Yesiree, those pumpkin cops were second.

Third, the townies. A shower of curses, *fucking commie queer nigger-loving fucking pinko kikes.* Fourth fifth sixth one-hundred-seventeenth the townies. Then beer bottles, rocks, broken glass everywhere, and then Shep and Louie yelling "Run! Back on the buses! Everybody, run! Sylvan Lake comrades, back on the buses! Fast!" I grabbed Sheppie's hand, still feeling his kiss tingle my lips as the Peekskill rabble-rousers cursed us.

Sweet Sheppie. Sir Walter Sheppie, ever the gallant gent, shielded me from harm, pulling me out of the crowd back toward the bus, covering me with his jacket.

As we headed for the bus, it started getting really serious. Rain, I thought, knowing that wasn't the word for what was coming our way. A young girl standing right beside me, a real Plain Jane, ordinary as mayonnaise, threw a rock at me as Sheppie hauled me up onto the bus. It hit my knee, ricocheting away.

"Tramp!" The mayonnaise girl yelled, pushing me into the bus.

"Commie bitchslutwhore! You suck Stalin. You filthy kike cocksucker." Her mouth was almost lipless, a pencil-mouth, spewing out long lines of hate. "You suck Stalin, you suck Paul Robeson's black cock, you and all your filthy Red sisters suck every nigger cock in Peekskill." Beer poured in one side of her ugly mouth and curses ran out the other. A bit of foam stuck to the side of her mouth as she yelled. "You go on your knees for Paul Robeson's black dick. You suck all the Jew boys out in your dirty commie tents. We gonna run all you commie kike cocksuckers out of Peekskill. Out of America! Fucking Yids. Go back on your pinko bus and suck your stinking queer kike cocks now," she taunted. Suck, suck, suck. This lady was obsessed with cocksucking.

Sheppie shook his fist back at her and yelled god knows what, but a crowd was suddenly forming around us, full of pencil people, flat-faced drunken men and women waving baseball bats and broken beer bottles, out for some fun. "Get the hell away from us! We got the right to be here, same as you!" I yelled out the window.

"Oh yeah?" A bat-wielding, peach-faced pencil man ran up the steps of the bus and stepped right up to Sheppie's face. (His face was exactly the color of your shirt, Simon: an orange peach.) I wondered, stupidly, where he'd gotten the bat. From his son? Or a neighbor's kid? Had he spelled it right out, "I need your bat, kiddo, to go beat on some Commie kikes?" A real shrimpboat, this nudnik. He oughta be dipped in cocktail sauce. Sheppie towered over him, all six feet of him pulling up in self-righteous rage, but the shrimp had a bat.

Sheppie pushed him off the bus, knocking the bat out of his hand. The crowd roared, ready for blood.

"Let's *move,* folks!" I said to everyone, pulling Sheppie up the stairs, inside the bus. The bus, the bus, it will all be safe on the bus.

Then it wasn't one rock but ten, then hundreds, a hailstorm pelting the rest of our Colony as they made their way onto the bus.

Where did so many people come from? The cops looked away or joined in. That's what our boys said later, at least. All I remember was that mean mayonnaise girl, the shrimpboat, the bat, and the bus. Later, we called it a pogrom and the papers called it a riot, but right then, nobody had a word for it. We were speechless. Except for Sheppie.

*

"You sit here. Come on, ladies on the inside, gents at the window," Shep insisted, with that phony English accent he used for flirting. I wanted to look, to see the ugly faces screaming and throwing and reddening as the driver turned the engine on and inched the bus out.

"Come on, Shep, I want the window seat. I need a view."

"What, you're the man tonight? Not with that hat!"

I pushed my magenta fedora down over my forehead defiantly, feeling cynical and strong like Marlene Dietrich. "Hat or no hat, I get the window seat."

We scuffled, forgetting about all the ruckus outside, two kids fighting over the best candy or the only unbroken cookie. I want, I want. He tickled, I pinched. But as always, Sheppie got his way.

"Here, you can have this. It's better than the window." He pulled a pack of red licorice from his pocket as we leaned into our seats.

"Okay," I conceded, snatching the candy out of his hand and trading places.

The bus tried to pull out without hitting anyone. Since I didn't win the window seat, I couldn't see them, but I could hear them. What a crowd. It was the usual litany, only louder, meaner than I'd ever heard it. *Nigger-lover, Jew commie queer, pussy, pussy, pinko faggot, Yid, dirty whores, kike-fuckers, nigger-fuckers*, and back to *nigger-lover* again and again. I leaned back in my seat. In one minute this will be over, I thought. Louie will pull the bus out, we'll hit the highway, and—

"My eye! My fucking eye!" Sheppie cried, blood pouring out all over his face.

One second we were flirting over red licorice, the next we were covered in blood and glass.

*

Is that how you got it?

Were you there, hidden between two Peekskill storekeepers? Was that you, one of those pasty-faced children, peering out from beneath his mother's apron, taking it all in? Did you yell, "Kill the niggers, fry the kikes," just like your daddy?

Peekskill: let's see, that was the summer of '45, eight-odd years ago. You would have been smaller back then, a kindergartner writing out your name in wobbly letters: S-I-M-O-N. Were you there? Did you throw the rock that hit the window that shattered into sixteen pieces that pierced Sheppie's eye? A torn piece of it, left on the pavement amongst the broken glass as the bus pulled away. Just a sliver. Oh the wonders of modern science. A new eye, Sheppie-gray. Sheppie-sharp.

The left one, it was. A miracle that he wasn't blinded, they said at the hospital. Eyes bleed heavy, but this was only a tear on the lid and a small scrape on the cornea.

What a miracle: just a scrap, a little leftover bit (scraped off from the floor of the bus by an informant? Eh

Sheppie?) and kazoom! You wonderboys grew a beautiful new eye. Just a slice of eye and (pardon the expression) in the blink of the eye, shazam! A new eye opens in another man's face. In that abandoned factory out in Queens, Teaneck, Great Neck, wherever the hell you boys work, there it grows. Voila!

I must admit, I'm impressed. What's your secret? Shake it all up, and you get a new eye, identical to the old one, just like Sheppie's.

I saw it with my own two eyes: Sheppie's eye, bright clear gray blue, with just a touch of yellow around the side of the iris. Sheppie's left eye in your right socket.

Two left eyes you have, then? Two Sheppie lefties. Does it make you clumsy? Are you seeing double? Are you seeing me as he did that night out of the corner of his left eye, snooping down my blouse even as the rock hit the glass, leering a bit with the right side of his mouth as the glass shattered?

*

A bit more of that Peekskill night comes back to me now. Someone else's blood poured on me. I was wearing my good suit, my office-gal special. Raspberry tweed, with rust piping and buttons. And the magenta Marlene fedora, slung over my forehead in what I hoped was a rakish angle.

"Holy Christ! They've shattered the windows! Duck!" someone yelled too late.

Warm blood trickled onto my stockinged legs. I shouldn't have switched seats with Sheppie, I thought.

Somebody, Mady maybe, cried "Let's get to a hospital!"

As the bus lurched away, stones and bottles breaking our windows, bickering broke out: *What, are you nuts? We can't go to the Peekskill Hospital. You think we'll have any warmer a reception there? Well, big shot, you got a better idea?* For a moment, as I dizzily watched Sheppie's blood trickle down my legs, I thought we were back at the Barn, quibbling at a meeting.

"Watch out, Sylvie's fainting," Sheppie's voice rippled over me. I looked up as I fell back, and saw his eye, swollen, bloodied, broken.

I came to, my head resting in Sheppie's lap. Someone had bandaged up his eye with a torn undershirt. It was quiet on the bus.

"We're heading for Westchester General, Bunny," Sheppie softly whispered into my ear, "It's farther than the Peekskill Hospital, but we got friends over at Westchester General," and I nodded. My head felt light, like it was floating over my body, every body, the bus, the road, the dark night, Paul Robeson, swing low sweet chariot, the peach-faced Peekskill ruffians. I floated in an endless black sheet of paper that stretched as far as the eye could see above the earth. And there I saw it.

*

Pay attention to this part! Whoever's listening, listen! This is the Moment, the grand moment of disillusionment. Of whatever is the opposite of what in the old days we called a political awakening. Listen!

*

We were fighting for the sake of fighting.

For the first time, I saw it. The self-serving silliness of it all. The futility of it. Of us.

There is no revolution coming to Peekskill, Great Neck, Teaneck, or any other neck. Not now, maybe not ever. No revolution in White Plains, Hackensack, Westhampton. And no revolution in Sylvan Lake.

It's all in vain. A distorted form of vanity, in fact, like a woman loving her face in a foggy mirror. Not just this particular squabble over Paul Robeson and the Negroes, or even the Union Square workers' march scheduled for later that week, but all of it. The protests, the strikes, the meetings.

Yes, the meetings.

Why? *Why* you ask?

Because they, the People, the Noble Workers, those tight-lipped squinty-eyed schnooks out there throwing rocks at us, the Great Proletarians, don't *want* our goddamned revolution. And those that do, or might, or should, well they can see how completely overpowered we little Yids are. In that black-paper night, my head resting in Sheppie's bloodied lap, it was all too clear.

Workers, Comrades: Listen but good. We are not their comrades. They are not our brothers. They hate us, in fact. It's the end of The Struggle. And we've lost.

I thought of the mayonnaise faces of those Peekskill women, so pleased with their Chevys and sofas, so eager to beat to the pulp any dirty kike commie who would dare to let a Negro in their clean white town.

I shifted in my seat, the weight of Sheppie's head heavy in my lap, my mind racing. Heads are odd. Look at this one: so big, so brawny and solid on the outside, but inside, there's only the same pulpy mess that fills the rest of the body. I stroked his hair, feeling the warmth of his scalp. No more heads, eyes, teeth should be broken for The Cause. Ganug. Enough.

*

That's all I remember.

I might have some of the details wrong. Maybe it was in the hospital that you got it. Yes, you sliced a little piece of Sheppie's eye from under the lid.

Or perhaps, even *before* you harvested his eye, you were watching us.

I don't know how, it's just a hunch, but yes, I think you were there on the bus, watching. Collecting data. Channeling it back to headquarters through some invisible something or other—a ray? a nuclear laser? some other ultrasecret supersonic beam?—straight into a room full of gigantic computers, buzzing and beeping to themselves.

ZZZZZZsssss.

Perhaps I could have stopped it, my finger piecing the lid back together, shielding the iris from your invisible gaze. Or maybe it was already too late; you already had us; the workers were not comrades. The eye was unnecessary, just a blue souvenir.

Well, it's too late now, darling.

*

"It's too late," I repeated, exhausted by my story. Simon was out cold. I curled around him, inhaling his lemony scent as I drifted off to sleep.

*

I woke up and in you were. In that way that makes me lose all sight and thought: in, in, in.

The details are so banal, but I'll relate them to you for the record. For your listening pleasure, as they say on WQXR.

*

I was on my back, legs spread wide. You were sitting up, rooted deep in me, straddling me like a go-cart racer, legs stretched out long in the opposite direction of mine, hands squeezing my breasts, manning the dials. Pump, pump. You came fast.

Ah but that's premature, so to speak: the second before deserves recounting.

You were watching my breasts, or your hands on my breasts. As you pumped in, out, in, in, I feigned sleep, kept my eyes shut. Did you see me? Didn't you already come?

You went slack. You went hard. It started again: pumping on one end, squeezing on the other.

You weren't a great lover. No siree. I didn't see stars.

It wasn't like with Sheppie: no dramatic build-up, no velvet touch, no tongue dancing elbow to toe. Delicate? Delicious? Decadent? No. No siree. It wasn't even like with Max, all furious motion. It was just pump in, pull out. And repeat. Again.

But there's something to repetition. I was, I am, addicted to it. To the power to make you do it and to do it with such stupid fervor.

*

Oh—and there's another incident I remember specifically.

Something nasty, that I'd like to forget, but I'll tell you, since it might turn out to be important.

*

I forced you. Three times.

*

The first time, you didn't expect it. You lay on your back, cock curled back up on your thigh and I took you. Twice.

Afterwards, tears dotted your cheeks. A flush crawled over your pretty sand-colored lips. Such pretty lips.

And I forced you again.

*

Or was it the other way around, Simon? Maybe you remember.

I lay on my back. A drop of blood dotted my clean sheets, trickling out of some unhappy organ. You spread my lips open wide like a cowboy, high ho Sylvie. And you straddled and pumped and pulled out (too late!). And rolled off and left me hurt and flushed. And I was eager to do it all over again.

Maybe I forced you first, and then you forced me. Yes, that's possible. I think that's right.

Well, whatever happened that time, it left a lot of blood.

Scarlet streaking the sheets. My blood on your thighs, too bright for menstrual blood.

Your hand made a fist and plunged in. Your eyes followed it there, watched it move in and out of me, clever gray blue eyes watching closely, not wanting to miss anything.

Everyone out, I thought weakly. But no luck, not this time. Your fist was in and opening, each finger poking inside me.

My finger found your belly button and pressed in, too hard. Sad button. Soft belly. I rubbed your stomach. Your taut young skin said nothing new to me. I missed the feel of a bulging stomach covered with gray hair. Max's stomach. What the hell was I doing here, with this stupid kid?

I pulled my crotch up to your mouth, rubbing your features with it, wetting them one at a time. Eyes, cheeks, nose, mouth. I held your shoulders down as you tried to move your head away. I'm stronger than I look. Mouth, nose, cheeks, eyes. Your mouth didn't open, your tongue stayed uncooperative. But no matter. I used the rest of your face, grinding until I dripped over your eyes, cheeks, nose, closed mouth.

*

Another time I remember: the night I read you Max's letter. Yes, that same damn letter I'd fished out weeks ago, only to leave it crumpled on the kitchen table in all the goings-on.

One morning, you rested your head in my lap and I read it aloud to you. I don't remember why.

"Listen to this, Simon. I think it'll explain a lot." What I thought it would explain god only knows.

"Dear Sylvie," I began, half-giggling. "I am surrounded by olive trees and gray skies. I've never seen such colors. Their stunning softness reminds me of your hair in the dark, its red dimmed to sienna."

I had to stop there, in mock-embarrassment.

"Such a poet my Maxie was, eh Simon?"

I read it and you listened, half-asleep, hand stroking my thighs, listening casually, sleepily, like this was a great good-night story.

"...I'm here in the Plaza Mejor, smoking a cigarette with the boys, watching a bunch of old ladies, hair covered in white lace, click-clacking across the street to the church in their ugly black shoes, the square kind like Mady used to wear. Look at them go. They remind me of the yentas on Avenue K hurrying off to the butcher's before Shabbes."

You gave out a little snore, but I didn't care. "We are awaiting our orders, relaxing for a day before we go join the men at the Front. I'm sick of goddamned Spanish, sick of watching the stupid old ladies going to their fascist church, sick of goddamned paella. I want a Nathan's hot dog, with extra mustard and double the sauerkraut! And I want you."

"This is the good part, Simon." I nudged you, but you were out cold. "I miss you, Sylvie, your hair, your hands, that last night out by the lake in the Colony. But I'm stuck in goddamned Spain, fighting the pigs. The sky is gray, bright olive gray, and your brown eyes are not here. I love you and I fight for you and all the workers of the world. Love and solidarity, your Comrade, Max."

You roused on the last line, yawning and stretching. Then you snapped the letter out of my hands, tossed it aside, and pulled me beneath you.

In, out, in, in. The repetition was still so exciting.

I turned the tables for once: with Max still in my head, I pulled you down to the floor, fought my way on top.

But then you got me but good. You were bugging me; I have proof. Yesiree, you bugged me good.

It was morning and it was sandy. In my bed I found

Max's letter, crumpled up, and sand. A fine red grit collected in the folds of the sheets. From which road did it come? From which long trek, out of whose gray office, in what government agency?

Bodies always carry the roads they have traveled. Dirt, grit, sweat, sand: the smallest particles cling tightest to the flesh. Travel dirt, I call it. It starts as sea-sand, making an unplanned journey from the bottom of the ocean to the unsuspecting traveler who picks it up under foot, bringing it home on the rush-hour train. By the time travel sand gets washed down in the shower, mixed with five-o'clock shadow and soap, it's turned to mere dirt.

Max's sands were the first I found in this bed. Orange and gold: street sands brought back from Spain, so far a trip for a grain to go. For weeks after he returned, I couldn't get the sand out, no matter how vigorously I washed him and his sheets.

I fingered the grit in those same sheets that morning after I read you Max's letter. It was a lighter, softer grain, the sand of an expensive beach. Where did it come from? Did they take him to Miami, Palm Springs, Waikiki, let his neck collect dirt from a dozen different beaches? Or perhaps they manufactured it, sprinkled it carefully across his clothes, inside his pants, to make him seem a hoodlum, or a budding hobo, authentically well-traveled.

I took a grain of it in my hand and rubbed it into Simon's chest. He groaned, a swoon of noise rushing out of him. It wasn't Colony dirt. The roads leading out of Sylvan Lake are made of muddier stuff: yellower, the color of the cheap mustard you squeeze out of a plastic tube over a toasted hot dog bun. I rubbed it in harder, dropping the grains across his chest, stroking him with his sand.

Simon pushed my hand away as I tried to brush sand onto his stomach. Imitating me, he rubbed my stomach, though there was no such sand on me. Still rubbing, he moved on top of me. His hands cupped my breasts, their tips lacing together in a loose cat's cradle, forming a finger-brassiere.

"Oh Simon," I gasped, hoping he would gasp "Oh Sylvie."

And he was in and I was under and I gasped oh Sylvie and a million eyes, a billion trillion ears, spilled inside me. He pushed in harder not crying out, mouth in my ear, tongue cold and hot and cold again, travel sand gritting my back.

He said, "Sylvia Rachel."

So he knew my Jewish name, too, inherited from Mama's dead-in-childbirth sister!

Such good bugs, such fine spies, such sensitive tapes, to find my hidden name!

XVIII. Night, Bonnets

When I awoke I didn't wonder. I didn't ask myself how he knew my name, or worry about what had knocked me out. That lemony tang still scented the air. I felt my burning head, the grit of sand in my mouth. But I didn't wonder.

Instead, I worried about the tomatoes. Were they burning? He was still inside me, a slug curling up in its shell. I'd neglected them for days.

Some books recommend that you cover the skins with a thick flour-and-water paste to protect them from those strong rays, but others argue for a more moderate approach, since the paste can alter the tomato's taste. They advocate for bonnets. Paper bonnets, to cover each plant.

Oh, the bonnet advocates are certainly a convincing bunch. A diagram in my favorite garden manual, the one that Burpee gives out for free if you order ten-dollars worth of seeds, shows a round tomato surrounded by a circular paper orb. They look like lamp shades, the green fruit a light bulb.

I'll make the bonnets today, I decided, pulling away from him, wiping away a bit of his sweat on my chin as he slipped out of me. Yes. I'll go into Lewisboro, to Porter's Stationer's, and buy a pack of construction paper in sky blue, sea green, grey gray.

The boy can help me. Boys are good at picking out the right colors for these things. I can show him how to draw two concentric circles, watch his eyes brighten as we cut, fold, and turn the inert paper into bonnets, lamp shades, paper dolls. I'll have him draw each letter of the alphabet, hold his hand tight around the scissors as he cuts and pastes. We'll have a day of paper.

We'll drive. I'll borrow Shep's old Chevy, and away we'll go, zooming down the Saw Mill Parkway. Next stop: Lewisboro. We can pick up some groceries in town while we're at it, and then head for Porter's. You'll be my nephew, one of Rose's brats, maybe the middle one with all the freckles. "This is Harry, my nephew," I'll announce to old

Mr. Porter, who will just nod and inhale on his wet cigar. I hate seeing the spit where he's been sucking on it, dripping off the dark brown tip. He's wrinkled, that Mr. Porter, a rotten old fruit with two blue pits for eyes. You won't like him. You won't like his smell: old cigars and piss, a messy men's room. I'm sure you've smelled it before in your line of business. But you'll love the paper goods.

We'll buy all the right supplies. Rubber cement in a molasses brown jar, tan wood glue in a silver tube, blunt paper-cutting scissors with red plastic handles, and caramel candies with cream centers that stick in our molars, in a shiny gold bag of fifty tied with a bright green taffeta ribbon. You like green, don't you, Simon?

And then I'll show you the paper. Eaton Fifty-Pound Cream, Strathmore Sixty-Five Pound Linen Matte, and my favorite, Eaton Sixty-Pound Ivory Gloss. What glorious names, rolling crisply off the tongue like the characters in those old English novels we'd read in high school. By the time we're through, you'll know each one, the differing feel of gloss and matte beneath your fingers, the merits of the lighter weights. And the gradations of color! The blacks: true black, charcoal black, grainy gray, smoke; and the whites: bone white, bisque, cream, peach cream, gray cream, pearl gray, bleached taupe; and your favorite, the multicolored rainbow pack of construction paper.

I think you'd like green the best. Just a hunch, but I'll bet I'm right. So let's make everything green: the tomato bonnets, your paper dolls, the alphabet. A green paper world, all cut out for you. Or you'll insist on cutting it yourself. I won't help; I'll let you figure out how to angle the scissors to make the cleanest cut. How to trace, how to fold. But that's later.

While we're at the store, finishing up our paper shopping, you'll talk me into getting you some extras: silver thumbtacks in a plastic packet of a hundred, a college-rule notebook with a forest green cover, and a yellow legal pad, with a stiff cardboard back. You'll love them all. You can saunter down the aisles, picking and choosing, examining boxes of number two pencils, testing the pink rubber erasers piled like pig snouts in a yellow bucket at the cash register. We'll pile through the whole lexicon of tape, from clear to masking and back again. Tape me to the moon, I'll sing as we dismantle a carefully constructed pyramid of silver duct tape to select just the right one, tape me in June.

Back home, we'll cut out yellow suns and purple stars, and tape them to the blue walls so that we have the whole sky in our kitchen. We'll do the bonnets next, measure each tomato plant individually with a yellow cloth tape measure Mama gave me. I'll trace out a circle within a circle for each one, but I'll let you do the cutting. Careful! Circles are tricky. We'll use clear tape to fit them around the tomatoes. Tomatoes in bonnets, what a sight. Like girls in graduation dresses, chubby girls blushing a deep orange as we dress them in green paper gowns. They'll stand still as we tape them up, careful not to break their rosy flesh as we work. We're hard workers, Simon, sweating up a storm under the garden sun. Even your tongue will warm under that sun.

Then we'll go inside, have what Rose calls an orange cow, a ginger ale with orange sherbet floating like an icy island in the center of the glass, share a spoon and trace out the letters of your name. I can see your grin as we spell it out, first invisibly, then with pencil, then with scissors: S-I-M-O-N. You'll mouth it, forming each letter, sounding it out one letter at a time without making a sound.

"Come on," I'll say. "Say it."

I'll hold your fist in mine too tight as we both look at the letters, each one a different color, the *S* and *N* both sky blue, your color, your sky.

But you won't say it. Your mouth will form each letter, your fingers will cut paper, you will kiss me, but you will not speak. Not your name; not mine. But for once, I won't care.

It'll be a paper day. You'll love it.

But how to get from here to the car? What if someone recognizes you? Or what if they see your bare butt scuttling up Danger Road, or pressing on the plastic seats of Shep's car? What happened to those trousers, those khakis? How can I explain a naked kid in a borrowed car?

*

For a moment, I hesitated, letting the paper fantasy blow away. But I recovered, and swung right back in:

I'll have to buy clothes for you first, dress you up to look like a nephew. You'll wait, I'll shop. Yes. No, no; it will take so long, schlepping on the 11:15 train in to the City, then hailing a cab to May's, then the big escalator ride up to the boys' department, and then choices, too many choices, so many different colors and sizes. A shirt, a tie, trousers, underwear, socks...how am I to know what size shoe you take? Of course you won't tell me if I ask; you'll just smile your half-smile, pink lips smirking, understanding exactly what I'm asking. I can guess the rest, but feet are hard to estimate. I'll go to all that trouble, only to get the wrong size shoes.

And what if you're gone by the time I take the 1:57 back to Sylvan Lake? A waste. I wish you were a chameleon, camouflaged against whatever you stand beside, your flesh flushing red against the plastic Chevy car seats, fading to a pale off-white against all those reams of paper in Mr. Porter's Stationer's.

Better to stay home. Better to stay at home and garden, Max would always say on Sundays, or on any day when I accosted him with a list of errands and must-dos. Better to garden.

*

I was tired, exhausted just from thinking about the trip. But then I remembered the tomatoes:

We must make the paper bonnets for the tomatoes,

trip or no trip. I probably have paper here already. Or I could make a quick run to the stationer's, dash in and out, hope you're still here when I return. Will you wait for me? Or vanish, leaving only a small dark piss pool beneath the tomatoes?

*

I watched you sleep as my head spun more paper delights. I loved to watch you anytime, but especially asleep in my bed. There was something empty about your still form, your blond head resting on the pillow, your steady breathing. Only your eyeballs moved, rolling back, forth, back beneath those pretty violet lids. You never snored, or drooled, or got up in the middle of the night to pee. I'm a light sleeper; I'd know if it happened, believe you me.

That particular night I stayed awake for hours, watching you sleep, whispering to you about Porter's stationery, tomato bonnets, the glories of paper.

As you slept and I talked, I noticed you had a new hair on your left nipple. It was darker than the others, borrowed from a swarthier body. Dark, black, curly, too long. I imagined pulling it, hard, oh, ouch, moaning for you. Put words and moans, sighs and little exclamations and half-words in your mouth—

*RRRRR*ring.

Your eyes rolled beneath the lids, two soft-boiled yolks sliding over easy beneath a thin layer of whites. I didn't pick it up. Who needs it?

You jolted awake. And grinned, one of those sly animal grins. The phone was silent and you were alive and awake and naked on my bed.

XIX. Whispers

But of course it rang again. Goddamn Nebraska.

"Hello?" I barked into the heavy black receiver.

Click, click. A male whisper: "She's on, Bill! For chrissakes, get the machines rolling!"

"Hello? Who is this?" My throat was tight. Who's Bill?

"You don't have to shout already, Sylvie! I'm in Teaneck, not Timbuktu." Rose was on her first Winston of the day, her voice all gravel.

"Sorry, Rosie. I thought I heard someone cursing into my phone. Did you hear it?"

"Sylvie, you're getting a little meshugge out there in the boonies. Listen, I've got some exciting news for you."

"How exciting? I haven't had my coffee yet." I stifled a giggle as Simon put a pair of my satin purple underwear on his head and made space-monster faces.

"What're you laughing about? This is serious business, hon."

"You're not expecting again, are you? Rose, you gotta stop trying for a girl. 'Cause you know you'll just end up with another boy, and then what'll you do—start a baseball team? Form a union?" He had two pairs now, pink and purple, flopping on his head. I twirled the long black phone cord around my finger as I talked, wrapping it around the wrong way against its preformed curls.

"Oy Sylvie. God forbid. No buns in my oven. We can't afford another. Though I wouldn't mind having a wee one to cuddle again. A girl. The boys, the second they're out of the cradle, they're racing around like monkeys. But listen, I can't stay on the horn here; I've got to drive Hesh to work, his car's on the blink, and then stop at the butcher's. But we may have a special deal for you. On a house. A real house, Sylvia! Not like that wormhole shack Max-God-Rest-His-Soul slapped together. It's a real steal, this one. A brick Colonial, with a covered garage and a sundeck."

Of course, a house. A quick solution to the "What are we going to do about Sylvie?" problem she and Hesh tossed back and forth around the banana yellow Formica table in their kitchen each morning. "Rosie, posey. Why do you keep hocking me a tchynik? I'm not moving. I'm happy here; we've had this conversation a zillion times. Ganug; enough already. Let's let it rest. Okay?"

"Sylvie, there isn't going to be a 'here' for you there much longer. The way things are going, they're gonna round up all the troublemakers, and who knows, a couple of harmless old yentas may get thrown in for the ride, if you catch my drift. Seriously, Sylvie, we're worried."

I could hear her tapping a pencil nervously against the banana Formica table, rat tat tat, rat tat, as she paused. King Simon stripped off his underwear crown, letting the pink bathrobe fall open, then cascade down to his feet. He stepped out and paraded naked around the table, circling me, dancing a little left-footed jig and singing silently to himself. I gave him a girl's giggle, high-pitched and flirty, laughed it out of my mouth.

"Sylvia? What's so damn funny? What, you wanna be hauled off by the Feds? This isn't a joke anymore, darling. You've gotta think smart, Sylvie. Max wouldn't want for you to suffer like this."

"Who's suffering? I already got a house, Rose. Not to worry, darling; the Colony's finished. Kaput. No more 'collective' nothing. The house is all mine, no strings attached. We're finishing up the paperwork right now; I got a lawyer and everything. No more Colony, Rosie; like I told you, they're closing it down." I knew they might be listening, but at this point, I didn't give a damn. Let them come. Let them do their worst; I'll just stay inside, wait 'til they'd gone, with their bugs, Nebraska, boys and spies and sands. "It'll just be me and my house. And my garden. Say, do you need any tomatoes? Or zucchini? I'm up to my ears in zucchini."

"I can get all the vegetables I want at Waldbaum's, even in winter. But listen, Sylvie. You gotta be practical. Just because some dirty Party lawyer tells you it's all over doesn't mean the Feds aren't gonna nail your ass once they get wind of Sheppie and the Barn and all that gang. I know all about those boys. I don't want to see you in trouble. You've gotta get out of there, now. I'm not kidding you, Sylvie mishpocheh."

I noticed a grace note of fear in her voice. The song was familiar: leave the commies, come to the suburbs, come on, Sylvie, be practical, but this note wasn't.

"Rose, you gotta tell me: did they talk to you? The Feds or something?" Simon danced in a circle, making silent Indian war whoops, pounding his mouth with his hand. I remembered my own brother Sol making the same gesture. Dead at seven of the whooping cough, forty-years dead already, that one, but still all his silly gestures stay stuck in my head.

"Rose?"

A pause.

I'd been waiting for this day, staving it off, planning and planning for it, rehearsing what I'd say, then deciding it will never come. Don't be paranoid, Sylvia, I'd tell myself in Max's sternest voice. They won't go after a two-bit housewife like Rose.

But that pause was the sign: they'd cased out Rose. They were moving in on her. On me.

"Well, no, not directly. But the phone is making weird clicks, and our mail was opened every day last week. And then suddenly it stopped. I don't know. Maybe it's just some local kids messing around." She was hiding something. Her voice was clipped, her words careful, deliberate, as if she was talking to one of the kid's teachers and she wanted to make a good impression. I could imagine her smiling as she talked into the phone, her chin stiff and hard as she over-enunciated.

I fished for some licorice in my purse. "Rosie, don't give me the business. You gotta tell me the truth. I know you're keeping something from me. You're a lousy liar, Rose." She sighed on the other end, oof oof, but she didn't respond. "Come on, Rosie. Tell me. I could really get in trouble here. Like you said, this isn't a game." Simon came up behind me and dug his hand into the bag of candy, grabbing three long licorice strands. He bit the ends off of all three, solving the problem of which to eat first.

"Okay. Well, a guy did talk to Hesh. Just some general questions: are we members?, do we know anyone who is?, why do I go out to the Colony if I'm not a commie?, are we fellow-travelers?, all that. That's all."

"That's a lot. You didn't tell them anything, did you?"

Rose paused.

A bad sign. Simon was gobbling down the last of the licorice, his tongue red, his teeth blushing pink. A very bad sign.

"Well, did you?"

"No. Of *course* not. We pretended we didn't know anything. That we thought you were living out there for the fresh air. Though we'd have to be real dopes not to notice all the low-life Reds crawling all over that place. Sylvie, listen to me. We'll cover for you now, but you gotta leave. It's bad. Real bad. And only getting worse. We want to help, but with the kids and all, we gotta be careful..."

A rare moment of silence passed between us. My stomach clenched at the thought of Rose and the kids and the Feds. I could see Rose and Hesh putting ties on the boys, clean shirts, trying to make a good impression, heading down the Jersey turnpike into the City in the white Buick, getting lost trying to find some strange office downtown.

I could leave.

For the first time, leaving took root in my mind. I won't really do it, mind you, I assured myself. I tried to erase the thought, but it left its stain.

"Okay, Rosie. We'll talk some more about this. I have to go now. Love to the boys and Hesh."

I hung up, before she could protest. Oh Rosie, what did you do to get such a crazy commie for a sister? And your only sister, your only family left, no less. I still thought of Rose as my family: not Max, not Hesh, not Rose's sons, either; just Rose. Us: the girls, the only ones left. Mama dead, Papa dead so long, all five of our brothers, all dead. Max deader every day.

Simon bit the tips of my finger, like a puppy gnawing for attention.

"Stop it," I commanded. He bit harder, on my right index finger. "Stop that!" I hugged him tight to my chest, smothering him between my breasts.

Grab him, I thought. Grab him now, before they take him away. Run away with him, jump any ship, sail your pirate out to sea.

You think it's so easy, eh Sylvie? Max's voice intruded. I ignored it. Max seemed very dead.

The boy gave me a petulant frown, a clown-frown, the corners drooping straight down in an inverted smiley face. The frown flipped over into a mischievous smile. He wriggled out of my grip, sat me down in a chair, and put his hands over my eyes. I kept them closed. I stayed very still.

Once, twice, around: something smooth, like string but thicker, softer, was wrapping up my finger.

Once, twice, again: he wrapped around and around. I loved it.

He tied a knot on it, a big flouncy bow. And pushed my wrapped-up finger in my mouth, between my teeth. I laughed: it was licorice. Wrapped up in candy!

And licked up. His tongue bit and sucked, nipping at my finger, nicking its side as he tried to untie and eat my licorice ropes. I grabbed his soft member from between the pink folds of my robe, and wrapped it around the index finger on my other hand. A ring of him. It was slippery, soft and pliable, a hardening taffy pull.

Just as it stiffened, the phone rang again. Goddamnit! I let it go, flapping back beneath the pink robe, and picked up the receiver.

I heard a crackling sound, like Simon's, and then a man's voice in the background, almost like an echo, far away: "Turn it on! No, dummy, that switch, no, not that one; the other one. The blue one, yeah. Shut up, we got her on!"

And then silence. No static. I said, "Hello? Rose? Who is this? Hello? Hello?"

Silence. And then ringing, as if I'd dialed someone else, and then instead of a voice, the ZZZsss again, but muted, far away.

Silence again.

I waited, but nothing happened. So I hung it up.

"I've had enough of this," I announced, and took the phone off the hook.

*

"Simon, who is doing this?" He was eating the licorice, tearing it up with his fingers into inch-length segments, then swallowing it down. He didn't look up from his work.

"Simon, this isn't funny. I need to know."

He chewed, teeth working over the licorice slowly, methodically. No answer.

"Okay, no more candy until you tell me." I grabbed the torn-up segments and squeezed them in my hand. They had an odd texture, like an animal's skin, waiting to be tanned.

XX. Baloney

Ringing, always this damn ringing, Mickey Rooney every morning now. I picked up, ready for the boys.

"Hello?"

"I'm coming for you," the voice announced.

Rose, only Rose, her Winstons graveling her morning voice, but still the words scared me.

"What?"

"I'm coming for you. We're gonna go to Coney Island, just you and me. The boys are at scout camp and I'm all alone here, sweating like a goddamn pig. So we're going."

"But—"

"No buts. I'll be there in an hour. Look, I promise I won't talk about moving, or our little problem with Nebraska. Just come. And don't forget your sunglasses!"

I shook my head as she clicked off. There's no arguing with Rose, once she's got an idea and the car keys.

Simon sat up, prick pointing toward heaven. We'd been playing in bed all morning. I grabbed it too hard, tightening my fist around the head. Grimacing, face red and sweaty, he twisted away and ran off to the bathroom.

When he came back, we lay together on the bed on our backs. I stroked his flat chest, smoothing down the sparse hairs. No moles. Why didn't they think to sprinkle a few, a dot there, a birthmark here? Perhaps you have an answer. No?

I stroked Simon's chest some more, poking my pinky where I would have placed a mole if I were the...manufacturer? Designer? Creator? Near the left collarbone. Under the right nipple. Below the belly button. My fingers decorated him with imaginary marks. He kept his face neutral, looking up at the ceiling, unflinching.

"Rose is coming to take me away. To Coney. You know, the Wonder Wheel, Bumper Cars, the Haunted House, Nathan's.

His face stayed flat. My fingers tickled his stomach,

trying to get a giggle.

"It's an amusement park, Simon. Don't you want to be amused?"

He frowned. Shallow lines gathered around his mouth. He'll make a dull old man, with two shining eyes stuck in a sack of wrinkles. Simon at sixty, unspectacularly old. I tried to picture it. But perhaps these boys don't age. They're sent back to the factory for repairs at the first sign of worry lines. Or simply replaced.

"We're going to Coney, to have a baloney," I sang too close to his ear. "To Coney, to *Coney*, to have a *baloney*," I repeated, overstressing the bad rhyme. He frowned, letting it settle into his face this time. The more sullen he looked, the louder I sang. His frown lines were deepening with each "Coney." Maybe they'd stick. Maybe they would dig so deep no mad scientist could repair him.

"We'll go in a car, a big white Buick. You'll love it," I insisted, imitating Rose, who was always insisting emotions upon her sons. He grinned, chub cheeks canceling the wrinkles.

"And you'll meet my sister, Rose. The old bag on the phone. Let's see, we can't do the Harry routine with her. I know: we'll tell her you're one of the Colony kids, whose parents ran off to Brooklyn to attend to some serious Party business. That'll shut her up. What do you say? We'll get sodas and hot dogs and beach blankets. You'll love it, Simon."

He smiled conspiratorially, all traces of the old man vanishing. Greed, pure and oily, like French fries hot off the grill, glinted out of his eyes. Greed minus guile: is this the sum total of innocence?

"Sitwell Avenue. Ocean Avenue. Coney Drive." I murmured the names into his ear, tousling his hair with my hand. "Mermaid Lane. So, whaddya say?"

He frowned, trying to wriggle away. The old-man face again. I tried a different tactic:

"We'll get you popcorn with salt and butter. And taffy apples, coated in *both* red candy and caramel. And of course Nathan's hot dogs, with mustard, relish, ketchup, onions, all topped on a steamed bun." I pinched his bare butt hard on "bun." He gave me a stony glare. "Anything you want, it's all at Coney, so get your baloney, Mister Coney."

A glint of lust edged his eyes. I kept on:

"French fries, golden and thick, still hot, with a red plastic devil's fork to spear them up. You can have as many as you like. Taffy apples by the dozen. Saltwater taffy, a whole paper box of them, in green apple and Georgia peach and blueberry blue," I slapped his ass, hard, on each "blue," "as your goddamned blue eyes, you blue fiend, you. So whaddya say, blue boy?"

He said nothing. Of course he said nothing. He smiled a shy smile, a question—what? who could tell with him?—hesitantly forming behind his eyes. I held him tight, singing "Coney," "baloney," over and over in his ear.

"We're going to Coney!" The words kept dancing as I rocked him, whole lists of voluptuous names waltzing across my lips, "Sitwell Avenue! The Wonder Wheel! Nathan's! The Cyclone! The Sea! By the *sea*, by the *sea*, by the beautiful *sea*! Pirate Simon, Pirate Simon, he'll go straight to Con*ey*!"

As I rocked him harder, other words raced me, dizzy words humming in my ear. Undertow. Lethargy. Corpse. A boy a dead weight whitening beneath my fingertips. My body underwater, twinning his, towheaded and bleary-eyed and tongue-tied and buried together knee-to-knee under the sea. You and me under the dead dead sea. A body with a body, lifeless, blameless, quiet.

These I didn't mention. I don't like to rhyme aloud. Instead, I bribed. "I'll buy you a sweet. Hell, I'll buy you a whole pack of sweets for the car. 'Travel sweets,' Mama used to call them."

His face lit up, chin raised, pug nose pointing north. I felt warm and maternal, like a kid holding a puppy in her lap. I took his hand in mine, and covered it.

*

The car smelled of lunch-box fruit. Unripe banana, bruised apple, and Rose's favorite: overripe plums. I'm sure her boys never ate a single one. No lunch-box fruits for Simon, I resolved: I'll only give him candy.

"Skidoo on in," Rose directed in her syrupy kid-talk voice, gesturing toward the back seat. I slipped Simon a whole unopened packet of licorice, whispering "travel sweets" in his ear as he awkwardly made his way into the back seat of her car. Don't join him! I had to be firm with myself. Don't slip in beside him. Don't whisper another word to him. Move to the front, sit beside Rose, don't look back. Ignore him as you would any other scraggly thirteen-year-old you were stuck with for the duration of a hot July afternoon. Pretend he's a goddamn nuisance.

I allowed myself only a quick glance back as I slid in beside Rose. "This is Harry Feldstein, Rose." Christ! Not Harry. Rose has a Harry!

"Pleased to meet you. I got a Harry, too! He's a bit younger than you, though. Popular name these days, eh? So Harry, are you comfortable back there? It's a bit crowded, I know. The boys left all that junk..."

His eyes were cast down, giving me a glimpse of the surface of his eyelids. The blue showed through, tinting the lids violet, echoing the purplish blue in his shirt. Where had he found that shirt? Max's shirt. I thought I'd gotten rid of it. He looked like a pale scarecrow with that fershtinkener shirt hanging out of his khakis. He held the licorice carefully in his lap, hands cupping the candy as if it were liquid.

"So he's one of the Feldstein boys, huh?" Rose squinted into the mirror, sizing him up. I nodded, looking out my window, watching the Sawmill Parkway rush us toward the City. "It's a pity, such long lashes on a boy..." she stage-whispered. I grunted and closed my eyes.

Sleep came, fast and stony. I dreamt of stone. Gray slate, a traveling rock ocean, paved over the Colony. Not just the dirt roads, but my house, Sheppie's house, the oak table, even the Barn. First the slate wave rolled into town, covering Lewisboro in stone, covering over the shops, the stationer's, the gas station. Then it rolled up the highway toward the Colony. The Barn, the Feldsteins', the Lake: all stone. When it hit my house, the dream and the slate turned molten, stone shot through with fire.

"Larva," I thought mistakenly, the right word for it escaping me. I was suddenly inside, in my kitchen, trapped, watching the clock as molten slate engulfed it.

"No," said Max calmly, sitting beside me in his chair. "It's stone, not fire. Don't embellish."

"It's larva, don't you see?" I yelled back as I ran out into the garden. But Max was already stone. Black stone, no color.

In the garden everything bloomed white. Freesia, apple trees, lilies of the valley, giant Easter lilies, honeysuckle, white roses, baby's breath. All the white flowers I'd never planted bloomed. We're safe here, I thought, not seeing Simon but feeling his feet touch mine. I inhaled all the white.

And woke up to Rose attempting to sail her Buick in between two fat black Chevy convertibles in the Coney Island Parking Lot. "Wake up, you two sleepyheads! We're here. Who wants to go for a swim?"

The ocean: so remote, so unhappy. White crests, a choppy sea. The water paced around the shore, waiting for a storm. Hazy, hot, and humid, as they say on "News and Views." As we walked down past the greasy hot dog stands toward the water, I fancied I felt the barometer lowering, the uneasy ocean singing *it's thunder time, it's time for thunder.*

Rose hit it off with Simon. As we walked, she chattered ceaselessly. She'd found her ideal child: a deaf-mute. "Harry, are you a swimmer? My boys are all swimmers. Stevie, he's a junior lifeguard now."

We spread out a blanket, an old graying muslin that I recognized as a sheet from Avenue J. Simon ignored her, digging vigorously into the sand with his hands in little groundhoggish scratches. Rose babbled on, but every now and again, she paused to say "You see, Harry—" or "*You* know how it is, Harry," or especially "Harry, it's just a whaddayacallit, a goddamned *disgrace*, doncha know, Harry," and he'd stop digging. And turn to face her, pouring his blue gaze into her flat brown eyes. It was enough to keep her going on forever. I lay on my stomach, trying not to listen, watching him groundhog into the sand.

Just when I thought she'd never stop, Rose stood up, pulled her sun-hat off, and fished through her handbag until a shower cap appeared. It was the same shocking pink as her bathing suit, but covered with yellow plastic daisies.

Popping the cap on her head, she announced, "I'm going in. Sylvia? Harry? You gonna join me, before the rain starts?" She looked like a melted candy, all pink and yellow, strands of bleached blond drifting out of the sides. Rose always was prettier when she added too many colors.

Neither of us responded, so, sighing heavily, Rose ambled off her towel, down into the water. She neither plunged right in, like Max would've, nor waded cautiously like me. She strode at her regular gait until a wave took her under, pink-and-yellow cap still visible beneath the surface. First doing the crawl, now the breaststroke, ignoring the waves, she swam with determination, eager to get her day's dose of exercise. She could have been doing laps at the Y for all she cared, so smug and snug she was in her pink cap, unperturbed by the ocean.

We watched her swim out, until she was lost among the other swimmers. I moved next to him, and pretended to help him dig his trench like a kindly auntie would, my palms scooping up great heaps of sand, faster and deeper than his. And then I kissed him.

His lips were peeling, and so were mine. An unspectacular sunset was dimming the sky to salmon. His teeth bit into me, tearing up my sun-dried lips. Peel it all away; let's be done with skin. The kiss turned us around, spinning us away from the ocean, back to face the parking lot, hot-dog stands, pavement.

My tongue dove in and found a pearl underneath his tongue. I licked it. Do tongues always come with jewels? I couldn't recall. No, Max's hadn't any, nor did Sheppie's sloppy mouth.

Simon's pearl tasted metallic, like nickel. I tried to pluck it out with the tip of my tongue, to harpoon it loose, but something kept it glued there.

Was it really a pearl? Or another device, a spying ear, a secret eye? I'll never know.

My tongue tried to dig out the metal pearl, but it disappeared. Dissolved? I don't know. It was gone, that's all I can say. Maybe it was candy. An after-dinner mint. Or a microphone. Or a pearl.

Simon squirmed away from my mouth, flustered and pink-cheeked.

Rose trotted toward us. She could have seen us, picked us out on the beach from inside the ocean, but then again, she was too happily self-centered for such spy tactics. In the water she thinks of water; beside her sister she thinks sister. "Out of sight, out of mind": Rose's favorite maxim. I could just imagine her thoughts as she ambled out of the water: well it was a bit choppy out there, now wasn't it, easier really to just do my crawl inside at the nice clean Y, but the sand is sort of nice on my feet. A hot dog would sure hit the spot just now. Oh, she thought as she waddled up the sand to us, there's Sylvie and Simon looking all hot and bored. I'll bet they could go for a hot dog, too.

"Want a hot dog?" Rose asked, smacking her lips.

Simon looked cranky, lips splitting with sun and kisses. He'd stopped digging, and was throwing sand with mild aggression at my feet.

"I said, you two hungry?" She could sense the discomfort, but not its source.

And I was hungry. Desperately, dry-mouthedly, gut-grindingly hungry. I don't like hot dogs, but right then I craved one, splitting out of its skin, the bun soaking up the grease.

"Come on, Harry; hot dogs," I called to Simon in

my bossy-auntie voice, and up we went.

We watched the ocean as we chewed. I really don't like hot dogs, I remembered as I tried to swallow the rangy meat. We were at an outpost of Nathan's they had set up right on the boardwalk. It was just a little aluminum cart, like the ones the street vendors use, but it supplied enough hot dogs for a whole beach full of hungry people. The man running the cart had an overcooked look to him, his pug face burned to an orange bronze. But he sure did have an amazing array of condiments.

It was the condiments that most interested Simon. He heaped spoonfuls of relish on top of chopped onions smeared with yellow mustard over blobs of ketchup. The dog was covered. The dog was drowned in a condiment sea. The dog was rescued, pulled out by his delicate forefingers from the overstuffed bun, wiped clean of condiment, and chomped down in three large bites. "Pig," I mouthed to him silently. He giggled.

I turned away and watched the sky go gray. Rose talked a blue streak, her words blurring with the sky, sun, condiments. Simon kept his bun open, despite the departure of the hot dog, and licked off the remaining condiments. When it was licked clean, he presented the bun to Rose.

"Ick! I don't want your slobbery bun. What, is he a retard, too, Sylvie?" Rose cast it into the garbage, and the day ended.

*

Simon slept in the back for the whole long trip home. Rose drove too fast, passing and dodging every which way.

My thoughts rambled as we drove, disconnected and salty. I'll wash him, hold him under running water until all the hot-dog grease is gone, burn out his circuits, wet his wires. I'll hold him steady and still and kiss kiss too hard until his lips grow cold and purple, solid steel. I accidentally hugged Rose's pet hamster to death when I was two. Does she remember? I wouldn't let go of it, even after it stopped breathing, grew cold in my grip. If I hugged it more, I was sure it would grow warm again. If I just hugged it a tiny bit tighter, I'd breathe with it, turn hamster on Rose and the rest.

I breathed in deeply as the car sped on, ready to turn hamster, ready to kill for the pleasure of resurrecting our beach kiss, mouth-to-rancid-mouth, right there in the back seat of Rose's Buick. Too sweet, your pretty mouth, all lemon and sand and spit. I held tight to the memory of that taste on your tongue in my mouth, as Rose rambled on about her new pine tree and hydrangea landscaping.

"Everybody out! C'mon, kiddos. I gotta go pick up the boys. Unless you're coming to Jersey with me finally, Sylvie. You know I'll be calling you to talk turkey about that."

I made a face. "Thanks for the lovely day at the beach, darling. We'll talk soon." We air-kissed good-bye, and I pulled my groggy body out of the car.

Inside, the house seemed too quiet. I opened a fresh pack of licorice, split the pack in two, and poured us some grape juice in wine glasses.

XXI. Sleepers

I love a good trance. Out cold, a fallen prizefighter, I'd lie at your feet. You could look at me for as long as you'd like.

And then suggest, in a calm voice that I've never heard before, that I strip down to my underwear and sing like a bird, swear like a sailor.

On the count of three, I speak. One, two: my lips mouth the words silently. On three, your voice, surprisingly deep, pours out of my throat. I open my eyes and speak to you. I tell your story. How you got here. What you want from me. Why you want it. Your words, your voice, my throat. Three, two, one: silently, you put me back under.

I shut my eyes and when I awaken, I don't remember a thing. Do I?

*

It was a few days after Coney, a cooler day, cloudy and humid. We were out in the garden again. I was the swimming pool, the calm cement floor, holding it in, protecting the soil. So still. I wasn't worrying, not then. Even though the color had changed, I didn't worry; after all, it's the paint on the bottom of the pool, the "floor" Max called it, that makes the water that alarming blue, not the water.

So even though your piss had turned from bright yellow lemon to a cloudy white, I didn't worry. I knew all about how it worked. I'd done the painting myself. I wasn't very good at painting, but I enjoyed it, sure. Every summer, using those long rollers, like real workers, we'd paint the Colony pool Joe'd dug for us behind the Barn. We'd give it a fresh coat of that special swimming-pool blue, so pale, so bright, so unlike any sea. I painted slowly. I'd get too much paint on the roller, was too heavy with my hand, gave too small a stroke. I did it all wrong, but I loved doing it. I loved walking on the floor of the drained pool, slowly painting myself into a corner. It felt like we were getting away with something, walking around at the bottom of the pool without drowning or choking.

So I knew not to worry about the color of the fluid. It's the color of the pool bottom, not what fills it, that matters.

I didn't mind that it was piss, not water, filling me up. Piss is better than water. It has more color, more substance to it. They say piss is sterile, which is more than I can say for the Colony pool. We were always having to disinfect it with chlorine, boric acid, ammonia, all sorts of stinky chemicals. But your piss was pure. And hot. And clean.

But it was different this time. Not just the color, but the smell.

As he sprayed it over me, the swimming-pool floor contracting with pleasure from breast to toe, I breathed in. Yes, something was off. Too strong, not lemony at all, more like turned milk. Hard to describe, those funny, pungent but not overpowering smells. I inhaled deeply, trying to identify the scent, find a word for it. Sour, that's it.

Simon felt very far away that time. He did it so mechanically. I felt a bit mechanical, too: not like a lover, the freshly coated pool embracing the water, just the swimming-pool floor sniffing sour pee.

And then he stared down at me, Shep-eyes going to soft focus, gold ring turning brown, lust blurring everything as he pushed his hard sour cock in to me.

In, out, one, two, three, I was out cold.

And you were gone.

*

And I'm still waiting for your lips with their soft anxious kisses to come.

Say the magic word, Simon, and wake me up out of this night. This unlovely world.

*

Three, two, one. Wake me up!

Like capitalism, some are more susceptible to it. A snap of the fingers, a flash of rhetoric, a certain glinty gaze. Any shiny object, any suave slicked-back hairdo. Even a wrist watch will do.

In a trance, you could keep me for a hundred years, a sheltered ivory princess locked in a tower of sleep. And then three, two, one, awaken me at will. Make me talk. Recite your words, bark like a dog, take off my dress. And then clap your hands and make me forget it all forever.

One, two three: perhaps I'll never awaken. I'll sleep as you count, your voice, your words, your will buried deep in my slumbering brain, waiting to be released.

Say the magic word again, Simon, and wake me up. Say my name. I know you know how. My Jewish name.

But it's not you who are keeping me here. Not now, anyway. It's them, always them, grubby gray-suited them, in various stages of unshaveness. You, you never needed a shave. And they're all solidly built, broad-shouldered men, not a boy among them.

*

There's more, of course. "Of course and always," Rose used to sing around the kitchen to the radio, "I always loved you, of course of course and always," chirping off-key to some invisible radio Valentino.

*

Of course I didn't know then that the night in the garden after the trip to Coney was the last time you'd come. That it was our last night together, though it only becomes the last now, as I look back from this stony cliff of the story. But that night. I didn't know. Pleasure unfolded around us, like a white piece of paper, no need for any goddamn words to spoil it. So I won't.

*

This story could be short: you came and you left.

Things were quiet. Without your silence, there were other kinds of quiet. Long nights of it, stretching into quiet mornings. And gardening. And pondering.

I had lots of theories. Maybe you'd just gotten tired of me. Maybe you were sick of my gifts. Yes, I thought. I gave him too much.

I could imagine your report, longhand, written quickly, lots of mistakes:

> Sylvia bot things and bothered me today. "Simon. New socks!" Why does she grab my handsr whenever she talks? Why not my arm?
>
> "Look Simon, a racing stripe! Did you ever see socks with stripes like that before?" New socks, new shoelaces, a haircombd, a belt: she likes to buy me accessories, presented in sky blue tissue paper with complicated folds. Why can't she get me something I need, like a Swiss army knife? I smilej a thank you to the socks, shoelaces, hair comb, belt.

There's more on the next page, typed, no errors:

> "<u>Simon</u>, <u>you</u> <u>want</u> <u>that</u> <u>we</u> <u>should</u> <u>garden</u> <u>today</u>?" Sylvia speaks as if she's underlining each separate word with a thick black pen, a pen not made for such purposes
>
> "Simon, how does my hair look? I put it up special for you." It's always Halloween in her hair. She fixes it half-way, but crazy curls escape from every side.
>
> "Simon, do you like it? It's called

a French twist." I smile, thankful that I'm mute, freed of the need to find the polite but truthful compliment.

"Simon, Simon..." Her day is chatter. White noise to me, the shika-shika of a truck routed for the long haul. The only pause is the silence when she comes. I love her then.

Sylvia wants perfect tomatoes. She wants the earth to stop rotating, the coin machines in the laundromats to pause mid-cycle, and my empty mouth to speak.

"...Nu, Simon, do you get it? The undertaker's underwear!" Sylvie, Sylvie, demanding a smile after each of her corny jokes. But she wants my silence even more, to dig a cave in her abdomen and plant it there and weed until it flowers quiet flowers.

Not a flattering portrait.

*

Or maybe it had nothing to do with me. Ha! Wouldn't that take the cake? Maybe you'd just decided to go back home, wherever that was. I saw that look in your gold eye at Coney. Remember? I do:

You pick up a clamshell and filch out the life with your index finger. No pearls for you, piglet! your stepfather would say if he were here, running a beery hand through Simon's hair.

You toss the shell into the sea, and run in, following the shell. A wave and a dive and you're under. Low tide, smelly sea. Like a restaurant, your father's, before they clean the floors at night. You swim beneath the surface, away from the smell. If your father were still alive and cooking, you wouldn't be stuck here.

You swim down to the bottom and grab a clamshell from the white fleet parked on the ocean floor, pretending it's the one you threw. "And if my grandma had wheels she'd be a street trolley," a voice mocks from somewhere, nowhere, the restaurant. You think of that ditty of Mo's: *Hitler only had one ball. Goering he had none. Himmler was similar.* You have two. But more hair there than you'd expect, dirty blond clumps of it. Himmler was similar.

The night you ran away you sang the ditty aloud in the shower, like your stepfather would, to the tune of "You Ain't Nothin' but a Hound Dog." You have a good voice. You have a long skinny prick you eye suspiciously in the shower. Why is it so long? The fat guy in Union Square last night said, "You can do well with that unit, buddy." A unit: you like that idea. You and your unit got out of the shower and loped across 8th and 43rd in search of a quick buck and a firm hand.

Now you're at Coney, stuck with the cow and the sister of the cow. You can hear them back on the shore: "Sylvie, darling, a little apple juice for you?" "Please, ganug already, Rose." "But Sylvie, you know how easy you get dehydrated in this weather. Remember that summer back in '38 when I had to carry you out of Klein's!" Sylvia ignores the face you make; she's absorbed in Rose's dehydration epic. Goddamn bitch. Your unit rises at the thought of the word "bitch" and you pull a piece of hair behind your ears. You look back at the shore, watching the cows talk, watching the men watch you. Sylvia's thighs bulge out from under her hot pink flowered bathing skirt, and she gives you a wink. Your unit is at half-mast. You see Sylvia's mouth move, responding to Rose, lipstick clotted in the lines. It's time to go home, you think. I'm sick of this kike food; I need a fucking ham sandwich.

*

Or maybe it wasn't the sandwich. They'd called you back to headquarters, convinced that they'd gotten all the information they needed. Th-th-that's all, folks! the boss cartoons a crow into the wire threaded special in your ears. You nod, you leave.

We'll never know which it was, now will we? All I know is you left.

*

Past midnight, I sat up in bed, watching your eyeballs fluttering under your lids. A long day at the beach; a restless night.

What to do? I folded some of the paper I'd collected from our Coney excursion: the wrappers from the saltwater taffy, the napkin you used to wipe the hot-dog grease off your mouth, the tissue Rose used to blot her fuchsia lipstick, put them in the drawer with Max's letters, and went to sleep.

XXII. A Nechtiger Tog

You don't worry much about light. It's just there or not there, in which case you say groggily to your husband, "Will you turn a light on already? You're gonna go blind, reading in the dark like this." You don't wonder about its origin. Who cares how they get it from the power plant to the bulb? Light is just light. And darkness is darkness: the opposite of light, no need to trouble yourself each night about how the world slips away, where it goes. No. You needn't pause as day fades; don't give it a second's thought. It's dark, or it's light. Until a nechtiger tog.

*

A hiccup of light, and then the long unbroken darkness. The world drained of color.

Is that accurate? Not quite.

Nechtiger tog, yes, that's closer. A nightly day.

Is this it? The A-Bomb? The H-Bomb? Another secret letter exploding? The end?

I waited to see if I was incinerating. There isn't any good language for that light, nor the darkness that followed. Dayblack. Deathnight. A nechtiger tog.

*

After it ended, I looked out my kitchen windows into the dark earth. No mushroom cloud, no scorched ground; just night. Maybe it's a new kind, then. A bomb? No, not a bomb, something even newer, stranger, stronger, developed for the Nazis, but mighty handy now for killing those stinking commies.

You don't ordinarily think much about light, or dark; light is just here or gone. Until in a second, an eighth of a half-second, a nechtiger tog.

*

For the record, let me just say this: it ruined my kashe varnishkes. I was boiling the bow-tie pastas in a big pot, and browning the buckwheat grouts with butter and onions on the skillet. I do both steps at once, boil and brown, no need to waste time. I like to cook, but only if it's over fast. "I dreamed I saw Joe Hill last night," I hummed as I sautéed.

It was midnight, my favorite time to cook. Our first years out here in the Colony, Max and me made midnight meals all the time, feasts of kasha and kugel and coleslaw, sided with sour pickles. It was such a delight to be free of the work week, liberated from the bonds of the workingman's lunch pail and the early dinner. We'd eat until two or three, stay up to watch the sun rise. And then make love with full stomachs and greasy fingers, and sleep in all morning.

*

That night, I was a midnight wife again. I wasn't waiting for you to awaken, exactly; I was just enjoying my cooking, hoping you would show up, stumble out of bed, and eat some kasha. As I lowered the flame on the burner beneath the buckwheat, there was the flash, and then black.

"Christ!"

My fingers fumbled with the burner knob. By twisting the knob on the burner, had I blown a fuse? But of course gas and electric don't share circuitry. I knew that. Of course I knew that. None the less, I turned off the gas, just in case.

Putting on my orange cloche, I looked through my window. Outside, it was only darker. *Could* it really be the Bomb? Whaddayacallit, with a bang and a whimper? But there was only darkness. A quiet night, crickets chirping.

In the bedroom, it was even blacker. I felt for you, but you were gone. Only pillows and a pile of sheets.

I walked outside in my turquoise bathrobe and cloche. Nobody would be able to see that I was wearing my fancy hat. The thought reassured me.

The trees brushed against my arm as I ran down my driveway. It took us a while to figure out what to do with all these goddamn trees. Shep got a book and started a nature class, so at least we knew what to call them. This is red maple, this is Dutch elm, that's hemlock. And of course you all know pine.

Red maple, sugar maple, ash. Rehearsing the names calmed me down a bit. The streetlights that lined the unpaved roads were dead. I looked down the road, towards the Barn. Black sky, black earth. Nothing but black.

Something was funny. The Barn! We always left the light on in the Barn; it was a Colony rule. But now it was black.

Of course. They've got the Barn.

All our heat and electricity were wired through the Barn; how, only Max and Louie knew. All the houses were joined together, connected by wires to the Barn. An electric bünd, we were. I'd seen it, the power plant lodged in the Barn's basement, an octopus of heaters and metal boxes and odd-colored wires. Our ferkakte generator, Max would say with pride, whenever the lights flickered in a storm. Don't worry, we have a backup system. It'll kick in, just wait a moment. And it always did.

But now it was dead. Somebody must've shut down the electricity intentionally. The backup generator, too. Somebody had taken over the Barn.

I thought of going to find the others. Go tell Louie and Sheppie, Max would have said. Come on, Sylvie, don't be a fool. This is serious business, if they've got the Barn. Let the boys know. No, Maxie. I'll handle it myself. Sheppie's not gonna bungle this one.

I turned around and headed back up the road to my dark house. I stopped for a moment in front of the empty Feinstein house. Their kid had left his tricycle on the lawn. All year it had been lying there. In the dark, it looked like one of those crazy modern sculptures, the kind that makes you think of a car wreck.

I thought of Simon. Perhaps his circuits were out,

too. A nutso thought: why would the generator in the Barn have any influence on the boy's circuitry, if in fact he even was some sort of a machine?

I was sweating under my cloche. Were the orange feathers getting wet? Was I having a hot flash in the middle of an explosion? Where should I go? To Simon? How could I find Simon, make sure Simon wasn't hurt?

My head cooled, the word "Simon" of all things restoring my equilibrium.

But how to find you? Where could you be?

I turned. I knew exactly where I was going: to the Barn.

*

Inside the Barn, it was even darker than out on the street. No light, nothing to break the dark.

Mm, h, mm, sh, ash, sh.

Two or three sets of lungs, hushing oxygen in out in. Also known as breathing. Max would've sighed if he'd been there.

I made my way to the meeting table; I could tell that was where the breathing was coming from. Tripping over chairs, I reached the body on the table. It sat up and smiled.

"Simon," I cried out in relief, rushing to hold him in my arms. I couldn't see his features in the dark, except for his toothy half-smile, the bright white front teeth digging into the bottom lip. "Oh, Simon."

Someone giggled in my ear. Or two someones: two identical young boys' voices, coming from either side behind me, giggling together. I turned around to see who they were but they knocked me out cold before I got even a glimpse.

*

Animal, mineral, or vegetable? Mineral, maybe. Rock-hard, granite smooth. Workers of the world, unite in granite! I was sweating hard, fingering your new metal mole. Yes, it could be mineral.

I had woken up, it was later, we were in my bed, home at last, and I was feeling your metal mole.

Mineral? Black granite. Or vegetable: think of where rubber comes from. Born in the heart of a tree. Extracted, mixed with thickeners, boiled, molded, and stretched; then dyed, cut, shaped, and shipped. But still a vegetable heart pounds inside.

Can they make rubber as hard as this? I touched it again. So hard. Placed right beside your lips. Why hadn't I noticed it before? Had it always been there? Or had they added it when they knocked me out in the Barn?

The lights were on, every light in the house. Outside, the streetlamps were lit all the way down Old Colony Road. And your face was alive and here.

Or was this a fake, a substitute Simon? Goddamn them. Goddamn them to hell. I grabbed him.

How could I? I could. I did. I pulled him closer to me, stroking his face, kissing kissing, pulling him on top.

Something trickled. Wet and warm, down my leg, over my thigh.

I'm wetting my bed, I thought with alarm.

I didn't feel like I was pissing, though. I fingered myself just to check. Dry as the Sahara, as Max used to sneer on occasion. Maybe something spilled. A glass of water, for instance, knocked over from the table beside the bed. But it was warm, this trickle, the piss-worm winding its way down my thigh. And it smelled like piss: not sour, not lemon, just piss.

Was it his? Do stones cry? Do rocks bleed? Do rubber spy boys piss? In my excitement, I didn't think of all the other times he'd pissed. If I could just figure out where this piss was coming from, I knew I'd finally know what he was. Animal, mineral, vegetable. Vegetable?

I grabbed the head of his thing in my hand, eager to find out.

What happened next?

*

Here's what happened: I squeezed the head of his thing, my index finger touching that hole. But there was none! Just the mole on his chin, and a bed full of his sour piss.

Loony-bin babble, isn't it? Bring in the men in white jackets. And disgusting, all this nonsense about piss. Bring in the morality squad.

But it's true. It wasn't you. It wasn't.

XXIII. Gone

Everyone knows zucchini doesn't demand much. Seed, soil, a can or two of water, and up they spring. Good comrades, those zucchini. They were our first vegetable victory, in our Colony garden behind the Barn, back when even our gardens were collective. So proud of those damn zucchini, we were.

My basket was heavy with their green uniformed bodies. I'd harvested too many. Who will eat them all? I examined one, grabbing it by the stem. The zucchini seemed to be still growing in my hand, its skin stretched too tight over the flesh. I would have felt lonely out there under the darkening mackerel sky, if not for the zucchini. Zucchini: now there's a good working-class vegetable. They have a simple proletarian wish: to make more zucchini. They have attainable goals.

This sky, though, didn't know what it wanted. I watched the sky change as I harvested the zucchini, squatting down with my pruning shears and wicker basket. Purple, orange, then gray pressed out of the sun, competing for supremacy. The scent of thyme was heavy in the air, like an amateur cook spicing the night with a single flavor. Goddamn zucchini.

I took a dirty hand to my face, feeling for tears. Yes, I was crying. I can't always tell when I'm alone. I have to touch my face, feel the wet skin under my hands, finger and figure whether I've moved from sad to tears.

"Simon's gone."

Saying it out loud only made it worse. I repeated it in my head: he's gone.

*

Did they come for him? Did you come for him?

*

It had been a week since the Barn incident, and I hadn't seen a trace of him. August 1, and he was gone.

The thoughts raced: Maybe they drove right up my driveway in a big blue van, pulled up and pulled him in while I was off at a meeting. Perhaps he's being beaten, right now, his soft skin bruising blue.

Or maybe he just left. Mission accomplished. If I didn't still have the red bandanna in my pantry, I would've started to doubt that there'd ever been a Simon. He took his khakis, so there I had only the bandanna, a sorry flag to wave.

The tears stopped. There was a small flat expanse spreading in the sky, a place where it was already twilight, a blue black hole. Was he swept up into the sky by some angry cloud, eaten alive by the night?

Something moved. Out in the hedge by the driveway, near the garbage cans in their wooden casing hand-built by Max to keep the raccoons out. Was it just the hedge reminding me it needed trimming, quivering in the hot wind?

I craned my neck forward. And heard it again. A rustle, with too much intentionality for a hedge. The sound of feet. Hiding.

I watched the hedge for further signs of motion, wondering if I should go out, investigate. I didn't even have the requisite flashlight, much less a trench coat. There could be more of them, a thin one placed behind the poplar tree, a fat one squatting behind the mulberry bush in the center of the yard. Herds of boys with blue gray eyes, the left irises all tinged with yellow. Should I wait them out? Should I hide? But where?

And then in a dash, a gray blur in a dark flannel suit ran for the road.

He was tall, close to forty. A thin man, with graying black hair cut close, and sharp blue eyes that darted faster than his feet.

And just as fast, he was gone around the corner, out of my sight. Back towards the road, the train, travel dirt from my yard following him back into the City.

I walked out to the hedge and investigated. He'd left big, flat-footed footprints. The earth was wet from an afternoon shower; the ground was ripe for footprints. And indeed, he'd left two deep gouges where he stood behind the hedge, most of his weight on his left foot from the looks of it. Smooth-soled shoes, office shoes. No good for line work or gardening. I retraced his steps in my head:

A man walks away from the train station in a gray suit and a darker gray hat. Broad-shouldered, with sharp gray blue eyes darting across an unexceptional face, he walks with confidence down the highway, not looking back to see the train station receding in the distance. No one saw him walk off the train, no one is watching him, no one pursues him, yet there is a distinct sense that he is walking *away* from the train rather than toward a specific destination. He carries a large black leather briefcase under one arm; under the other he clutches a square composition notebook patterned in a mottled black and white. A schoolboy's notebook and a businessman's briefcase: an odd combination. It's the only remarkable thing about his appearance, really. His head is bent towards the ground as he strides away toward Route 22. He is walking *away*; this much is clear.

When he hits the unmarked, unpaved, easily overlooked turnoff that links Old Colony Road to Route 22, he turns, not onto the muddy unpaved road itself, but into the thick side brush that lines the shoulder. He bolts.

There is no moment of hesitation, where one can see him ask himself "Road or shoulder?" He heads straight in, clutching the briefcase a bit tighter to his side, picking up the pace, not worrying about scuffing his shiny office shoes. He's still walking away from the train, yes, but now he's also walking toward something.

It is hot and unpleasant, all those scratchy weeds hitting his face, bugs buzzing up against his sweaty brow, as he rushes through the bramble at the side of the road in his good gray suit on this humid August day. But he keeps up the pace, ignoring the bugs and weeds and dirt as he dashes. He's heading backwards, wrong way, away from the train. He follows Old Colony Road.

My house isn't the first he sees. First, he passes the Feldsteins'. Theirs is closer to the road, and larger than my Sleeping House. It's painted green and white, country bungalow-style. A friendly house. But the Feldsteins' is clearly empty. It's not just that they have no lights on inside; outside, there is no telltale sign of life: no garbage can spilling over with the remains of a meat loaf, no gardens, the lawn unmowed. It takes so little time for a house to look empty. Only the bicycle left rusting on the lawn proves that it was ever inhabited. The man in the gray suit looks carefully around the Feldsteins' property. Their house is starting to sag; the paint is peeling off in green chips, and grass infests the driveway.

Obviously empty. The man looks down the road, at all our empty houses sagging against the road, and walks away from them like they're a pack of stray dogs he hates feeling sorry for. Fuckin' dirty commies, he thinks. We're just giving them what they got coming.

He walks on down Old Colony Road until he hits my driveway. He can see the mowed lawn, the glow of a working kitchen, the well-weeded garden. And so he goes to the side hedges. They line the driveway, giving it a sense of entrance. One of Max's Spanish whims: a driveway with tall trees he wanted, a row of poplars meant to evoke cedars, planted on either side. The royal touch, Maxie joked. But the poplars didn't survive that first winter, so instead we lined it just as carefully with hedges.

Perhaps it is this sense of entrance that invites him into the garden. They must be the leaders, he thinks; they have the nicest house. And get a load of this landscaping! Those commies are such damn hypocrites; they preach a good line, everybody getting the same deal and all, but look at these folks. They're living the life of Riley out here! He is looking for a big catch, and he sees our hedges and thinks he's found it.

Or perhaps he is looking for Simon.

Perhaps he's Simon's father, coming to find his runaway son. He has the same square chin, the same hard glare to his gray blue eyes. And that stoop, shoulder rounded, chin jutted, one hand on his hip: Simon's assertive slump. What would the mother look like? A blonde, a pretty washed-out blonde, with plump lips she embellishes with fuchsia. He gets his lips from his mother.

Where's my son? the man thinks, scrutinizing the landscape. The man's cold eyes survey the house, taking in each detail: the bright kitchen lights, the red hammer-and-sickle clock, the recent paint job. He is still absorbing each detail when our eyes meet, his eyes widen, and his feet flee.

Or is he the stepfather, out for revenge, ready to drag that fuckin' kid home and kick his sorry ass from here to Shanghai?

Or is he a spy? They've warned him: don't get caught, don't let those commies catch you. They're dangerous, those reds: they got guns and gas stockpiled in those old bungalows.

I didn't know. I don't know. Still, I saw him. Ha!

*

But I didn't see him first.

They told me about it at the meeting:

A man walks away from the train station in a gray wool suit and a darker gray hat. Broad-shouldered, with sharp gray blue eyes darting across an unexceptional face, he walks with confidence down the highway, not looking back to see the train station receding in the distance.

No one saw him walk off the train, no one is watching him, no one pursues him, yet there is a distinct sense that he is walking *away* from the train rather than toward a specific destination.

He stops in my hedges, no need to repeat that part, and when he meets my eyes he runs down the road until he reaches the Barn. It's closed, no lights on inside or cars out front. It has that odd presence of a house unpeopled.

He comes out of the bramble, and stands in front of it. He stands there, just stands and stares, until he notices someone is watching. And then he dashes into the brush, and vanishes.

*

I'm sure you have lots of stories about the man. You would enjoy telling the story. How it began. How he came. How you came. How he came. How you both left. Oh, you'd tell it with relish:

I seen him following me. I don't know when he started—coulda been right at the bus station—but I seen him tailing me not three feet behind as I pushed through Union Square. I figured he was just another perv scouting for action. I seen them plenty at the bus station, following me into the can. At Sixteenth Street I stopped and turned around to face him. "Hey pops, who you starin' at?" But instead of scurrying away, this guy stood and looked square at me.

"Sonny, you look like you could use a hot meal," he began, moving towards me like he was gonna pal me on the arm. "Whaddya say we go—"

"Aw, brother. Take a hint, go chase fruits somewheres else before I call the fuzz on you." Not like I would be calling the coppers, since they'd as likely kick my ass back to Lewisboro as nail a perv.

The man laughed, pushing his glasses farther up on his nose. Nerd glasses, like Jerry Lewis, lying thick and heavy on his narrow face. "Ho ho. So you think I'm some nancy boy. Ho ho ho. That's a good one."

Goddamn fag. I hadn't heard a ho ho ho like that since Christmas. I turned to make my getaway into the crowd.

The Santa fag grabbed me, pulling the shirt collar

off my shoulders. "I'm no perv, buddy. I got a business proposal for you, okay?" He didn't look like Jerry Lewis no more. I noticed he got a beard sprouting every which way around his chin, and a glaze to his eyes. He pushed his glasses again. "You look like you could use some easy moolah, now couldn't you, brother?"

I looked him straight in the eyes. He was a big guy, with big eyes and hands. Blue eyes, like me. No yellow cat's eye on the left one, though. Only me and Sheppie got that.

I tried to wriggle away, but he kept his hand gripped on my collar.

"You want something to eat? How 'bout spaghetti and meatballs? We'll go to one of those Village dives and get the works. A bottle of red, a beer or two, and a big plate of spaghetti," he grinned. "My treat." His teeth were a moony white, but the front one was chipped. No, this one's no perv. I felt in my pocket: three quarters, one dime, and two nickels. You can't get half a lousy meatball with that.

He smiled that goofy smile again and kept pushing up his glasses. I decided to like him. "Okay."

Bugs? Secret documents? Mrs. E. and the Colony? Nah, they were later. First came meatballs...

*

Your voice would trail away, like an old trade route growing over with ragweed. You would save the rest of the story for later. For the meatball man himself, perhaps.

XXIV. Watching, Watching

Sheppie spotted him next. It was at some stupid goddamn meeting, after the Big Meeting where the Colony dissolved itself, and after the meeting after the Big Meeting where they'd sold the Barn to the highest bidder, some goy from Lewisboro.

I'd been boycotting, first staying home with Simon, then staying home waiting for Simon, but Gladys insisted that I come to this one, "One last time, Sylvie, come on, just once more, we need you. It's about the electricity, and the ownership of our houses. Please, Sylvie. We've lost Elaine and Joe already. We really need you." Always that same line: we need you, the Party needs you, the Lincoln Brigade needs you, Rose needs you, the Colony...

"Alright, Gladys. This is my last Mickey Rooney, and that's final." But of course it wasn't.

*

It was hot in the Barn; my eyes were closing, remembering your hands. Sheppie was babbling on about god knows what when he stopped and gasped. "A man is watching us outside," Sheppie said in a low voice. "Crouch down. Don't move or breathe or talk."

We crouched beside our folding chairs, like obedient children in a duck- and-cover film. I sat on my knees, noticing how dirty the Barn floor was. Louie peered out the window, reporting. "He's coming out of the bramble from the side of Old Colony Road. He's crouching low, like a robber or something. Now he's walking across the front lawn. Damn! He's behind the Barn now, in the bushes; I've lost sight of him. Stay still: he may be watching us."

Despite Louie's admonitions, everyone began to whisper: *do you think? could it be? I told you so, keep still, would they really? I warned you, hush up, what now?* As I sat, knees smarting, I thought of telling what I'd seen. Who I'd seen. And yes, what I'd done. But how to explain it all? So I kept my mouth shut. He'll be gone soon enough, I thought, shifting from my knees to my bottom.

I was right. He disappeared without a trace. Sheppie and Louie walked around the Barn while Gladys, Mady, and I waited. Just us three girls left. They gossiped; I brooded about your hands. Then the men checked all around the Colony, and found only footprints. Big flat footprints, from a large man's feet. Only footprints.

It wasn't the first sign, of course. We knew by then we were being watched. We'd all heard weird clicks on the other end of the phone, opened our mail only to find it already opened, noticed an odd metallic taste in the water. We didn't even bother to call it Nebraska anymore.

We got up off our knees and went home. What else could we do?

*

"Emergency Mickey tonight, Bunny," Sheppie called me up later that afternoon. "We gotta do something about that creep who's watching us."

"You want me to do something about a Peeping Tom? Please, Sheppie.

I got better things to do," I snorted.

"Bun, this is serious. This stinker is more interested in chasing commies than skirts. Come on, help us out here. Come to the meeting. Pretty please? Look, I fixed the Barn generator all by myself the other night. But for this I need you. Come on, Hon-Bun. You're always good at coming up with plans." He was flattering me, but it worked.

So I went. With my orange cloche sweating in the early August blaze, I marched to the meeting to talk about the man.

But as it turned out, that wasn't what the meeting was about.

As usual, they talked about everything under the sun except the sun glaring in their eyes. Shep was harping on the gravel in the spinach.

Oh, sure, Sheppie mentioned it, as a side dish to the spinach, "So make sure to wash all your greens real good. The cars are kicking up gravel, like I said, and if it got in my spinach, you can bet it'll get in yours. And be careful, folks; we're being watched. We saw a strange guy staring at the Barn again the other day."

Nobody reacted. Nobody was surprised by the man. Nebraska was everywhere, every day. Phones clicking, strange voices clearing their throats at the other end. Strange blond men in gray were spotted at the stationer's, at the train, outside our houses. The surprise was in how erratic our Peeping Toms were, how haphazard. Just like us!

You'd think we would've been panicked. And sure, some grew fearful, some left. Take Elaine and Joe. But they'd left quietly. You'd think we'd have talked of nothing but The End, what to do, where to go. You'd think we would have thought of nothing but the terrible possibilities. Of the Feds, HUAC, the Chair. Interrogations, blacklists, blackouts.

But we preferred trivia to trauma. No matter what new nonsense occurred, no matter how tangible the evidence that they were closing in on us became, we stuck with the usual petty mishegas. Even I was guilty.

And this time, spinach was the hot topic, gravel and spinach and cars, which twisted back and forth around the issue of whether to pave the roads of the Colony or not. "*Karl* goddamned *Marx* said nothing about dirt roads. *Vlad*mir goddamn *Le*nin said nothing about dirt roads. So who the hell decided dirt roads were Party policy?" Gladys groused. I thought of Simon, and the day we burned the spinach and jumped on the bed.

Argue, argue, complain. Mady was raising her voice at Shep: she knew spinach better than anyone, she carped, and the dust blown from the dirt roads was making it sandy. "Listen to common sense and pave the goddamn roads already!" The men were adamant, though. No pavement.

And then Shep saw it and said it. "Shh, there's a man out there, watching the Barn. Christ! He has a gun. I can see it in his hand. Goldenrod, goldenrod! Everyone shut your traps and duck. This isn't a test," Shep added, for whenever Mady started in on one of her rants, someone else was likely to "run a test" and send us all into hiding with "Goldenrod" or even just a quick "Gold!" But we knew it was no test.

"He's in the front again. Just staring. Gray suit, gray hat, black briefcase. Black pistol. Smart shoes. Oh my god, he's writing in a notebook. It looks like he's making a sketch, from the swooshes his hand is making. HUSH THE HELL UP everybody!" We hushed, the silence of anticipation, like an orchestra tuned and ready to play. "He's like some ferstunkene schoolboy, scribbling away in that composition book. Lined, probably. Jesus. A goddamned kid they send us!

"Okay, he's walking away now. Turning up Danger Road." Shep whimpered. He knew what was next: a rap on the door, interrogations, turncoats, the wife left alone crying. Or worse. Since he was a commandante, a bigwig Party leader, and their house was the only house still standing on Danger Road, he figured the odds were looking like he was the designated well-cooked goose. They like a mascot, those boys at the FBI do.

Or was he in on it? The golden eye, the file, even the fact that he was the one to sight the man...Shep could always cry a crocodile tear or too. Well, then he played it good, he did. A command performance. "Christ! He's coming closer. Shut the hell up, everybody!"

*

We stayed there until morning. Someone made tea, sweetened with molanus, frozen raspberries brought out of the storage freezer and sunk into scalding water. No one slept.

I drank my tea fast, wishing it were my coffee, my kitchen, scooping the boiled raspberries from the bottom with a teaspoon, eating them hungrily, even though I didn't like their texture, too seedy. What if Simon came back to the house, and here I am, sucking raspberries in the Barn's basement? But I had to stay. Who knew what those FBI kooks were up to?

*

In the morning we walked Shep and Gladys up Danger Road to their house. We walked together, in a row spread across the street, singing the "Internationale." It was too late to hide; we might as well sing. "So comrades come rally, and the last fight let us face, The Internationale unites the human race." There were only five of us, hardly a whole race, but that didn't stop us. We kept singing, crooning "Solidarity Forever" and "My Yiddishe Mama" with equal militancy. Shep was the only one who could carry a tune.

In front of the house, we paused. Louie and Shep checked things out, while we waited, still singing. "Unites the whole human race," Shep and I harmonized on the end.

"Well, no sign of entry, not even a strange footprint or two, though it's hard to tell on these dirt roads," Shep reported. He scratched his arm; I thought of Simon's scabs. So symmetrical.

Inside, we waited. Gladys made more tea, more raspberries. A coffee cake was brought out, dry and smelling of the refrigerator, but we ate it greedily. And waited.

The phone didn't ring. We waited together for an odd hour that lived somewhere between a ladies' coffee klatch and a union strike. Nothing unusual happened, and once it became clear that nothing more was likely to happen, the decision was made (I don't remember by whom) to leave. Return to normal. Pretend nothing had happened. Sing the "Internationale" one more time. Worry about spinach and strawberries.

*

I stayed. Gladys seemed jumpy, and someone

needed to help her with the dishes. And since Simon, bygones finally were bygones, at least by my reckoning.

After we'd rinsed everything and left Shep to do the drying, we walked out into Gladys' cornfield, as we often did back in the old days. It was a small clearing in the side of her yard, with no other vegetables planted in the vicinity, more grove than field.

Shep and Gladys had decided back during the war that it was a scandal for the Colony to buy our corn from the local farmers at their nickel-a-bushel stands by the train station. Gladys made a huge issue of it, called a special Corn Meeting. "We're two years out of the City already and what, we're acting like factory bosses, exploiting our comrade workers for pennies? No, I don't think so." When nobody contradicted her, she stomped out of the meeting and went off to plant sweet corn, the white, small-kerneled kind, in a small patch in her yard. Their house wasn't even finished yet, and even the Sleeping House was still a bunch of bricks, but she insisted we grow our own corn.

They were small, just an inch or two larger than those baby corns you get down in Chinatown. Adolescents, you might say, awkward pale yellow, full of silk. More silk than corn. Late bloomers, too. September was their season.

*

So the corn ears were just beginning to ripen on that August day when Gladys and I investigated. They were closed up tight, like pursed lips, the kernels inside rock hard.

We walked through the ears, grown high, above our heads, not speaking. Gladys suddenly pulled a stalk down, seemingly at random, and held the ear across her palm for inspection. Somebody had already done the same thing, for the ear was opened, the silk pulping out.

"My corn," she announced without anger. "They've been in my corn."

Now, it could have been anyone. Any old schmoe could have come along and opened up an ear of corn for kicks. But who would do such a thing? Who besides a Colony member even knew of this corn patch in back of this dead-end house on Danger Road? Who would bother? The corn wasn't even ripe. She was right: it had to be him. Which "him"? I thought of Simon, nonchalantly eating Gladys' corn raw, his bandanna around his neck like a farmhand.

"I gotta go, Gladys. What if he's gotten into my garden? Or my kitchen?"

For once, Gladys understood. "Okay, Sylvie. Be careful. Don't let those gray bastards get you."

The Sleeping House was empty. Nobody had come. Nobody came.

I inspected my garden carefully. The tomatoes were almost ripe. The books had lied! Piss didn't kill the tomatoes, no indeed; it seemed to have actually fertilized them.

"It just goes to show you, doesn't it? Don't believe everything you read," I muttered the clichés in a Rosie voice.

Or maybe the piss was poison. That lemon scent, yes, of course. I'll bet it's a rotten trick. They look so good because they've been slipped a Mickey. I wouldn't put it past them.

I pressed my finger against the skin of a ripe one, tapped it, brought my nose to its perfect flesh. Sour and clean. Red and juicy. Piss and poison.

XXV. Rose Red, Rose Green

There were more sightings after that. We stopped reacting, stopped hiding, stopped, in at least one sense, worrying. Reports of random man-sightings were circulated:

A man appears by the Lake. He's standing on the boulder at the edge of the shallow beach. It's a favorite rock, the one the kids used to lie on. He watches the water closely, as if expecting something to pop out and shake his hand. He waits.

And then, as nothing moves except the sun glinting off the yellowy water, he starts to talk. Well, not exactly talk; he moves his mouth in the shape of words, but there's no sound, like a silent movie.

There were two eye-witnesses: Mady and her cousin visiting from the City, Phil Whaddayacallit. They were in the bathhouse, changing for an early morning swim, when Mady saw him standing there. "Shuddup, everybody: there's a strange man on the rocks."

Shut up! He was in gray again, same hat and briefcase, same glittering gray blue eyes in a plain face, but no notebook. He seemed to be muttering words into the left pocket of his suit jacket. He bent his neck at an odd angle, making his chin flesh buckle up into folds. And then he jumped off the rock, walked out the gate, and headed down Old Colony Road.

"Come on!" said Mady, still in her bathing suit, gesturing for Phil to follow.

So they followed him, scurrying in their bathing gear through the brush at the edge of the unpaved road, trailing him all the way along the highway down to the train station. They watched him scurry up the platform on the Manhattan side just as the train pulled in, muttering curses under his breath.

And he was gone. Nothing was found on the beach.

Shep made Mady, and even poor Phil, out at Sylvan Lake for the day just to catch a bit of fresh air, recount the story separately. Their stories matched.

*

The third time was not the charm:

A man appears in my garden. Gray hat, gray suit, glinty eyes, no briefcase, no notebook. Dirt visibly soils his white starched shirt. And I don't see him.

Rose, always Rose, saw him first. She scared him away, I'm sure, with her cackle.

"What, so you're planting men in your garden now, Sylvie?" she joked as she slammed the sliding-glass door closed. "Maybe you'd like to grow me an extra, too!" I was making us coffee, trying to decide if it needed another minute. I came to the door in a flash, thinking it was Simon. He's back! Oh god, don't let her see him naked. Don't let Rose ruin it like she always does, with her dopey remarks and schoolgirl giggles. I closed my eyes a second before I looked out, expecting the worst.

But nothing. Nobody was out there. Only the heat and the tomatoes, waiting on their stakes.

"There was this man out there," Rose insisted.

"A man, or a boy?" I asked carefully as I poured the overperked coffee.

"A man. Some pervert in a fancy-schmancy suit. I oughta call the coppers on him!" Empty threats, her specialty. Even Rose wasn't that stupid; even she knew cops would be the last thing we needed.

"So did he have anything in his hands?"

"What?" Rose gave me that annoyed look, furrowing her brow and screwing up her face in disgust. The lines of her eyebrows looked drawn-on in the kitchen light.

"A briefcase? A notebook?"

"I don't know. There's a strange man in your garden, some ferkakte Peeping Tom doing god knows what, and you want to know whether he's taking notes? You're nuts, Sylvie."

I didn't answer. She knew what I was talking about.

I just looked away, and we sipped our coffee in sullen silence.

"Nuts," she muttered.

*

It was hot in my garden. Or was it me? The hot flashes were getting the best of me, turning on the ovens behind my knees under my arms across my brow. Broil! Rose had finally gone, so I went out to investigate.

I spied a red object planted in between two zucchinis. Simon's: his bandanna. Who stole it from my pantry?

Picking the bandanna up gingerly, I tied it around my neck, and wondered what to do next. It was strange to wear it. I sniffed: just a faint aroma of dirt, tomatoes, sand. No lemons.

I walked inside wearing the bandanna, following with my feet the path your eyes would take you. The piles of books on the floor, the old radio in the corner, the hammer-and-sickle clock. It's hard to imagine anyone cooking here. What a mess.

*

The last time I saw the man, it was a bit of a disappointment. For one thing, it was over so quickly. For another, I wasn't sure it was him.

I was walking toward the Barn to get some ice, and he was walking away from the Barn, toward my house. I noticed him because he looked a bit like Simon, though much taller, and because of the snake.

It was pink, a horrible fleshy color, and it moved like a writhing intestine around the man's wrists. The man walked forward purposefully, in big jerky strides, but he wasn't making much progress, since he had to stop every few feet to wrangle the snake. Its skin looked moist, like maybe it had come from the lake, perhaps some sort of eel.

They were struggling: the man trying to keep hold of it, the snake wiggling around. He didn't notice me at first, he was so preoccupied with the snake.

When there were only a few yards between us, I stopped. I didn't want to catch up with him. I hate snakes. And besides, it annoyed me to see a boy so similar to you, same eyes, same peeved expression, same hair, but so many years older. Dummy, he's a man, not a boy. Not Simon. A relative, perhaps?

Simon's father?

Simon's boss?

The man stopped, too. He looked at me. I fished my glasses out to see who it was, to make sure it wasn't a Colony oldster back for a visit.

It wasn't a snake. I walked closer, though he stayed still. It was a tube, a pink rubber tube, connected to a small black box in the man's other hand. The box was vibrating, making the tube move.

ZZZZssss. That sound!

"Hey!" I called out. "Hey, mister!"

His face froze, and then his feet ran. He darted off the road into the woods, shoes crunching the bramble underfoot. That's the last I saw of him, you, until now.

*

I'm sorry. I'm getting ahead of myself again. Where was I? Oh yes, Rose and the Conversation.

XXVI. Move

"You have no muscle," Rose declared, her eyes searing over my bare arms. I glared at her, hugging my arms to my chest.

"It's because of the Change, Rose. You'll see soon enough." I smiled our mother's tight smile, warding off further discussion. But not even Mama's smile could stop Rosie.

"Oh, Sylvie. It's happened already? So early? Why didn't you tell me?"

"Well, it hasn't exactly arrived yet. But there are signs."

Rose gave me the smile now, a frostier version than Mama ever used. "Oh, you and your signs. With your harlot hair, anyone would think you're a goddamn gypsy." She opened her light brown eyes wide, as if to emphasize the difference in our coloring. Her hair was bleached a lighter, yellower shade of blond than usual: some New Jersey hairdresser's notion of shikse beauty, no doubt. It didn't suit her.

I rolled my eyes and kept hugging myself. Just to annoy her, I pulled an unopened pack of licorice sticks out of the pocket of my housecoat and started to unwrap it.

"All I'm saying, Sylvie, is that especially if the Change is starting, you should lay off the sweets. You don't want to turn into a butterball, now do you?" She grabbed the licorice sticks out of my hand and squeezed them tight, as if trying to slim them down, too.

"What, it's not enough to tell me where I should live, now you're telling me what I should eat? I'm fifty-three; I'll eat what I want." I grabbed the candy and waved it at her for emphasis.

She laughed, but snatched the candy back, opened her gigantic patent leather pocketbook, and shoved them in, a buried treasure.

"So Sylvie. We need to talk," she announced, grabbing my hand too tight with one of hers as she closed her purse with the other.

"Isn't that what we're doing? Talking?"

Rose laughed again, a snorty horse laugh. She has two laughs, my sister Rose: one for men, a coy giggle that swallows itself at the end, and a horse snort for the girls that begins with a honk and ends in a surprise sigh. She ended with the sigh this time, a long and wistful one. "Uff, oy, Sylvie, you silly dill pickle. I mean *talk*-talk. But not here." She looked down at the floor, as if someone might jump out from under the rug. "In my car."

"Why? What's in your car?" I asked, and then mouthed "IS SOMEONE FOLLOWING YOU?"

Rose raised her fake eyebrows and mouthed back, "NO – BUT YOUR KITCHEN IS BUGGED FOR SURE."

"IS THE CAR BUGGED?" I felt like I was in a play, one of those old Yiddish Theatre routines with the loud stage whispers.

"NO – HESHIE SAYS IT'S CLEAN."

Aloud, she said breezily, "Girl talk. You know I only like to have girl talk in the car."

"Okay," I said, as though this made sense.

We marched out the front door silently, walking down the driveway to the road where Rose had parked her Buick. The tail of the car stuck out onto the unpaved road.

Inside, her car smelled of chlorine and oranges. An odd combo, but easily traceable to two sources: her son Alfie's Thursday night swimming lessons at the Y, and Rose's passion for buying fruit in bulk and then keeping it in her trunk to ripen.

The plastic seats sighed as we sat. Inside was even hotter than outside. I tried not to think about our trip to Coney. I slouched against the seat, noticing something pink at my feet. Ice skates? I pulled them out from under the seat. *Pink* ice skates. In summer? Rose didn't skate, and had no daughter. Probably she picked them up at a yard sale, unable to resist the siren song of something for nothing. I thought of Simon on ice, a solo skater.

"So, where are we going?" I asked, locking the door and rolling up the window. "Hackensack? Timbuktu?"

"This is serious, Sylvie. Hesh thinks they're on to you in a big way. The man has been coming by the office again. And now he's really snooping around, asking everyone all about us. About the Colony. About you."

I fiddled with the lock, pushing it up and down. "Does he have weird blue eyes?"

"What? Who?" Rose took out a pack of Winstons and lit one up. The air in the car turned hazy, as if we were sitting inside a cloud.

"The man. The one you said is nosing around Hesh's office. What kind of eyes does he have?"

"How the hell should I know? What kind of meshuggeneh question is that, Sylvie? The Feds are sniffing us out and you're worrying about the color of some schnook's eyes?" She laughed the coy laugh. "Sylvie, listen. This is serious. It has to stop. It's bad enough now, but think how much worse it'll be if they nab you. For all of us: me, Hesh, the kids. Even if you don't give a damn about yourself, think of us. Of the kids..."

Kids? For a moment I couldn't think who she meant. Simon? I thought of the feel of his travel sands on my back, his scab beneath my nail, his golden eye heavy with sleep. I could feel my eyes closing as Rose went on and on.

Simon is listening.

I startled back into consciousness. He was close by; I could feel it. Crouching somewhere, maybe across the street where the forest meets the road.

I could smell him through the walls of the Buick. Lemon and sweat, and something else, something sharp. I sniffed: yes. Simon was crouched in the underbrush, listening, smiling at all this crazy talk. He was waiting for us to finish, so patient, so sweet, nibbling on a lone red licorice stick he'd found stashed away in his khakis.

"Sylvie? Sylvia?!" She was shaking me awake. Rose the Impatient. Rose the Non-Catnapper. "You're falling asleep on me, at a time like this?"

"Uhh...I'll see what I can do," I mumbled.

"'Do?' What you can 'do' is leave. Now. Most of

those old Colony shtarkers have already left, anyway. Even Joe and Ellie! Come with me, today, Sylvie, like I've been saying. We can sell that damn shoe box of a house later, Hesh will set you up in Jersey and sell it off in no time. Forget about those troublemakers. Live like a normal person for once, and everyone will forget all about this."

She lit up another Winston, smoking as fast as she spoke. "You're not a wild-eyed kid anymore, Sylvia. This is serious. You're practically an old lady already, going through the Change, no less, and here you are, still putting us through hell for some crazy commies. I won't take it anymore. Me or Hesh neither. Do you hear me, Sylvie? Do you hear one damn word I'm saying?" She sucked furiously on the cigarette, inhaling down to the filter. No one smokes faster than Rose.

My finger fiddled with the radio dial, the smoke or the Change making me nauseous, fingering the knob without turning it on. Maybe he's bugged this, too. Maybe it's transmitting Rose's exasperated sigh straight to headquarters. Lucky you, listening to this bupkes! "I hear you. Believe me, Rose, I don't want any trouble, either. But I can't just leave. There are other factors..." I groped for the word, gesturing with my right hand, searching for that one right word that would make her go away. It didn't come, so I kept my mouth moving. "You know. Top secret. Government matters."

That was it: government. The magic word. The code for "I'm a turncoat, Rosie. You got nothing to worry about anymore. I'm working for the other side. For Officer Friendly, the Feds, the whole goddamn PTA."

"The government?" Rose's forehead crinkled.

I looked down. The pink skate lay in my lap, cradled, a steel piglet. I don't want to be here, trapped in this car lying to my own sister, breathing her Winstons, loving up her skates. I want buttered peas. Peas, fresh from my garden, shelled and blanched, a pad of butter buried in the center of the bowl. Peas are a bore, except when they're fresh and cooked only a minute past raw. But fresh peas from my garden, sugar sweet and bright green? Heaven, darling. I'll bet Simon's never eaten fresh green peas, just those gray canned imitators. My nose wrinkled just thinking of their wrinkled skin, their tinny odor, pale impostors.

"Sylvie, don't make that face. You can't lay one on me. I don't believe for one minute that you have anything to do with the right side of the government. This FBI guy, or whoever he is, snooping around Hesh's office—he spells trouble with a capital *T*," she said, tapping the steering wheel with her index finger, the cliché spilling out of her mouth with a gust of smoke. Peas, butter, and a dash of lemon. You hear that, Simon? Lemons, for Simon-Sour-Pie!

I had to get rid of Rose. "Look, Rose. It doesn't matter what you believe. Like I told you before, the Colony is over. Dissolved, kaput. This is just a house now. I'm in the clear. Some of Sheppie's boys are finishing up the paper work, smoothing out the rough edges. Once it's done, nobody will know it was ever here. I talked to my...contact; he says I'm clean. No more Colony, no bugs, no Feds. Just me and my Sleeping House. These will all just be, be, country houses, nothing more. A country manor, Rosie! You can brag to all your friends about your rich sister Sylvie with her fancy estate." We turned our heads and squinted towards my house, trying to imagine it in its new life as a country manor.

But the Sleeping House didn't oblige. The upstairs had been built too hastily. It loomed uncomfortably above the foundation like a bird squatting on the wrong egg. Sure, with a fresh coat of paint and a two-car garage, this house could pass for a suburban split-level. But a country manor? It would take more than a coat of paint for that. No matter what we called it, it was still my crummy old Sleeping House. As we stared at my house, a lie sprouted beside it. "I know that guy, the one coming around to your office. I'm, um, helping out. The Feds. So you don't have to worry, Rosie."

"Oh Sylvie, you old fool." Rose glared at me, pushing back her straight blond bangs. "You think it's that easy to shake them? Feh! Sylvie, you're such a child. These FBI goons got records. And tapes. And judges in their pockets. They got everything. Giving the names of a few minor-league idiots won't save you. Sheppie's in it big, they want him, and they'll use you and anyone else to get him, and bring you down with him, no matter what line he's giving you. That Sheppie Goldstein. He's the cause of all of this. If only you had never gotten mixed up with him! They're hauling him in, Sylvie." She was yelling now. I looked away. She'd never said anything about Sheppie and me. "And if they want to haul all *our* asses in, they will. Including me. Including my boys. As long as you're living in this house, in this, this, *Colony*, you're a sitting duck, and so are we. Goddamn you, Sylvia. Your ass is grass, and Hoover's boys have the lawn mower."

I groaned: another of Hesh's dopey wisecracks had made it into Rose's stockpile. "Say I do what you and Hesh want. I move to Teafly or Teepee or Peepee, New Jersey, make nice with the neighbors, plant some petunias, bake a few apple pies, and what, suddenly the FBI goons just disappear? You think they can't follow me straight out there, right to your doorstep? They got files, Rosie." I thought of the green file Sheppie had tried to find in my house. Was he a turncoat, too? "Just like you were saying: they got tapes. Records. Everything. My only chance is to stay put, to look like I'm not afraid, tell them what they want and be done with it. Listen, Rosie. I could become a perfect capitalist pig with a cherry on top tomorrow, buy a house in Teaneck, join the goddamn PTA, and still the goons in the gray hats with the sharp blue eyes would be after me." I paused, realizing how loud I was shouting. When you're in a car, a little shouting goes a long way. "After you, too, if it suits their fancy."

Rose lit another Winston, even though she was still holding a half-smoked one. "Sylvia. Listen. Listen good, Sylvie. *We will not go down with you*. Or defend you. Or deny anything they accuse you of. Listen to me. Unless you get the hell out of all of this," she gestured all over, wrinkling her nose up, as if even the smoky air inside her Buick was contaminated by Commies. "And I mean all the way out, pronto-Tonto, no kitchkying around this time. They will come for you. They've told us. And, and we will do nothing to help you. We have to protect the kids. Look, Sylvia. They're closing in; there's no fence-sitting now."

Fence-sitting. A funny choice of words to come from Rose's lips, considering. Back in the shop, sitting around the lunch table behind the sewing machines, wolfing down our salami sandwiches, Bella and Rose would always get into it. "We need to take up arms, overthrow the bourgeoisie, topple the bosses, I tell you," Bella preached to the mostly converted.

Only Rose bothered to argue. "You people have no sense of proportion. You talk like the bosses, the 'capitalists,' don't got mouths to feed, feet to shoe, gas bills, too." Rose the Skeptic. Rose the Realist. Rose, always ready to argue.

"Strike breaker! Class traitor! Fence-sitter!" Bella would squeal, her face reddening as she launched into an off-key rendition of "Which Side Are You On, Boys?", substituting "gals" for "boys" on the appropriate lines. Sometimes Rose would respond with her own out-of-tune opus, either "My Country 'Tis of Thee" or "The Star-Spangled Banner."

I'd eat my salami sandwich quietly. I didn't defend or attack my sister. Bella knew which side I was on, anyway.

And now here was Rose singing that old song, but in quite a different key.

"For chrissake, Rose. I can't believe you're using that old fence-sitting routine on me. You do what you have to do; I understand. But I'm not leaving."

"Well, I am. And I'm not coming back here, Sylvia. This is it."

I sighed. I knew she wanted a scene. She wanted me to yell, "Well to hell with you," and flounce out of her car, or come docilely, tearfully into her arms, wrap my arms around her and her Tenafly fantasies, "Thank you, Rosie, for saving me," but I wouldn't give her any of that.

"Well, you've gotta do what you've gotta do, Rosie. I'm not going anywhere, so if you want to find me, you know where to look."

She said nothing, lighting up with one hand and starting the ignition with another. I squeezed her cigarette hand and let myself out of the car.

It was cool outside in comparison. Instead of walking up the driveway into the house, I ran to the garden. There were no footprints, no signs of Simon, no strange men, but the earth was so dry that nothing would leave its imprint.

I watered each plant, making sure not to drown anyone. It was a long afternoon; I was grateful when it was too dark to continue.

Inside, everything was quiet. Too quiet, too dark. I turned on all the lights, washed up, and made a small salad and a bowl of buttered peas for my dinner. The phone didn't ring.

XXVII. Marigold Joe

And then it did.

If I'd been fully awake, I would have hesitated. I'd have paused for a minute, allowing the phone to ring its way back to silence. Certainly I'd have turned on the light and checked the clock before picking up, wondering who the hell was calling at 3:37 in the morning.

But I was only half-awake. Hot flashes are like fevers, awakening you only half-way. I hung between awake and asleep, bathed in the flash, my shvitz of sweat.

3:37 a.m., and there I lay, drifting back toward a moist sleep when the phone rang and rang. If I'd been awake, I would have waited, but in my daze I jumped up into action.

"Hello?" Once I spoke, my head cleared and the worries began. Who would call at such an hour? The kitchen clock said 3:37, that's how I know when it was, its red face barely discernible in the early morning light. Who the hell would be calling at 3:37? Rose. Maybe something horrible happened to Hesh, a stroke God forbid, or her weak heart caved in, or one of the boys had an accident, or—

"Lovey?"

And then, "I mean, lovely. Ha ha."

Click. A hang-up sound, without a dial tone to follow it.

Laughter filled the background. Simon's giggles. But that voice hadn't been his.

"Lovey?" The voice again, questioning this time. A boy's voice, yes, but not Simon's. It was higher, breathier, and younger than Simon's uneven growl. Even though I'd only heard him say two words, I knew Simon's voice like my own mother's.

"Yes?" I answered, happy to be Lovey.

"*Be careful,*" whoever it was said, stressing each syllable. More giggles, the conspiratorial cackles of two silly boys, Simon's gruff half-laugh, I heard it distinctly, heh heh, and someone else's. Whose? And then the click again, and a dial tone. I waited.

Nothing. Dead air. Reluctantly, I hung up the phone.

I put the kettle on to give my hands a mission. Who was Simon with? Another boy? Another spy? The boys from the nechtiger tog?

*

A party, a tea party, with the blackest tea from China, no sugar, served with toast and marmalade, that's what we need! I brewed a whole pot. Tea for two, or three. I cut a lemon into six even slices and set it on a yellow plate.

There was a lot to do; tea parties don't make themselves. I poured three cups, and added a cube of sugar to each, except for the last. No sugar for my sweet Simon; he prefers lemon. He likes flavors that bite back: raw green tomatoes, tea that's half-lemon, red licorice. Lemon black tea for you, unsweetened coffee for me, I sang silently, brewing half a pot. I added an extra squeeze of lemon to his, stirring it in to the yellow teacup with exaggerated flicks of my wrist.

The yellow dishes: my inheritance, my victory. I fingered the rim of the cup, gloating. Not a banana-y yellow, no siree. More like marigold. And no design or special pattern. But they're real, pre-War china, and they were Mama's. A wedding gift for Mama and Papa, from a distant cousin back in Bialystak, a wealthy wool merchant who disappeared during the War: maybe to the camps, maybe to New York. Who knows where? Mama would say.

Rose got Mama's finest clothes, the ring with the real ruby, the wedding portrait, the furnishings from her cold-water flat, but I got the marigold dishes. In that hot summer of '33, as we watched and waited for the breath to leave her, sobbing around her bed, Rose's eyes passed quickly over the dishes as she made a mental inventory of what she'd take home after shivah was sat. I was too busy with the arrangements to care. But when it came time, Rose had already decided. "You take the dishes, Sylvie. Mama would have wanted you to have them." Actually, Mama wouldn't have wanted anyone to have anything of hers. She would have preferred to have been buried with all her possessions laid out around her, like an Egyptian princess waiting for a boat to row her to her proletarian paradise. But Rose took everything, leaving only Uncle Joe in his heavy wood frame above Mama's bed, and the marigold dishes in her pantry.

Stalin we never exactly discussed. I just took him with the dishes, shoving him into the same box. And once I took him, I ignored him, sitting on my kitchen wall above my phone, guarding the house like a Catholic saint. They say now he's a bad man, they used to say he's a hero, but I just think of him as Mama's Joe. His was the only picture she ever hung. Uncle Joe, her favorite and only surviving son. Uncle Joe, scowling out of that frame, protecting her from Russian dybbuks who might have come over on the boat with her, from fat American bosses busting the union, from Papa in a drunken rage.

Uncle Joe is failing at phone duty, I thought as I sat at the table after the phone rang, watching Stalin scowl, waiting. But then again, the phone did sit quietly for the rest of the morning, so maybe Joe was on the job after all.

I sat, not drinking, letting his tea and my coffee grow old together. I waited patiently with my three yellow cups, the boiled water for my absent guests cooling in the morning air. Time speeds and stills at that hour, like an ocean in which you can't chart distance, since here and there are the same. I stirred and waited, sleep carrying me slowly back.

*

I woke up to a bright day, sun full in my face, my back aching from my night in the chair.

Who's here? I wondered, seeing the three tea settings laid out before me. I was sitting upright, my head leaning to my right, my hand still grasping the teacup full of coffee. My back hurt, the sun glared, my head swam. And then I remembered the calls, the phone, the boys. Simon, he's here, watching, somewhere.

I opened the pantry: empty. I remembered our first night together, the bandanna, pirates, lemons, nipples.

"What do you want?" I said aloud. My voice was dry and raspy, like a cough translated into words. I sipped Simon's cold tea to soothe my throat. No reply.

Outside, the tomatoes were already scorching from the high-noon sun. Everything was stilled, as if some fickle god had stopped the spinning globe for a moment with the tip of his finger, and might start it twirling again just as easily. Nobody was there.

The phone rang. I picked it up, but it was dead. No dial tone; nothing.

I slammed the phone down, flushing with rage and hot flashes. "Goddamn you! Goddamn all of you!" Screaming always made me feel better. I'm like Papa that way, or the little of him I remember.

I cleared away the dishes, eyeing Stalin with a weary glance as he stared out from his frame. Watch it, buddy, I thought in Max's voice. Be careful. You better, whaddayacallit, *be careful*.

XXVIII. Good-bye

Later in the morning, what time it was I don't know, after I'd drifted into a light cool snooze, the phone rang again.

This time I woke right up and answered it, "Hello?", hoping for Simon, or even the other one, but it wasn't them. It wasn't Rose, either.

"Hello Sylvie, and good-bye."

Gladys, saying good-bye? Why?

"Good-bye? Whaddya mean, 'good-bye'?"

"We're leaving. Didn't Sheppie tell you?"

Like Sheppie ever tells me anything but lies. "No, darling. When?"

"The movers are coming in an hour. I could swear Sheppie said he told you. We're moving to Teaneck, remember? So I only have time for hello, good-bye, and do you want my table. It's the oak, the one that we used to have in the Barn. You know. It's too dark for my new living room."

"Today? You're leaving today?"

She answered with a babble of details: it's for the best, we can be more effective workers for the Cause in Teaneck, the movers, the lawn, the boxes, the oak table, blah blah blah. I stared into my coffee cup, the details swimming in my ears. Gladys is leaving. And Sheppie. Goddamn you, Sheppie, sending Gladys to tell me.

There was a pause: my turn to talk. "When did you decide to go?"

I didn't listen to her answer. How did it end up like this? Gladys and Sheppie, Joe and Ellie, all leaving.

First to join, first to leave. Ha! Bourgeois pigs. Teaneck! What low-life class traitors would run away to Teaneck! Or was Shep in trouble? Maybe Rose was right. Who knew what she knew? He'd break easily; always a talker, my Sheppie. I could picture him grinning that empty grin behind bars, eyes glinting blue and gold and hard as he told all. "No, Bunny wasn't in on it; it was all Max's doing." Or was he a turncoat, jumping ship now that he'd got us all in deep? "Bunny—Sylvia Edelman—she's a fellow-traveler." I could just see him cooking my goose, payback time, oh yes.

"...and oy the dust on those books in the attic I cannot tell you. So, Sylvie. The table. You want it or not? I can have the movers run it over to you before we load up the van. But don't do me any favors, darling. If you don't want it, I'll just leave it where it is. But the movers'll be here soon, half an hour or so, so I gotta know now."

"Well, I don't know where I'll put it, but I can't let a good oak table go to waste. So bring it on over. And I want to say good-bye, anyway."

"Oh Sylvie. It's not good-bye. We'll be back for," a pause settled inside the phone line. What would she possibly be coming back here for? The whole point was to escape, to pretend the Colony never happened, to blend into the scenery in scenic Teaneck. Or maybe they really were joining some meshugge group in Russia, and Teaneck was just a cover. Gladys in Russia! Gladys the Good Comrade. Sheppie's Gal Gladys. Gladys the Trouper, following her man over the cliff of his choosing. "...for all sorts of things," she finished vaguely. "But let me run that table over to you as soon as the movers get here, and we'll have a quick coffee klatch."

"I'm out of coffee, but full of klatch," I replied.

"Oy Sylvie, still such a card. Well, keep the 'klatch' warm; I'll be over in a jiffy. Buh-bye!"

Buh-bye, you turncoat, I thought. A tear formed in my left eye but not my right. Half a cry for Gladys. I was surprised to feel even half-sad; after all, it was Gladys who'd stood between Shep and me, literally stood there, planting her feet between ours at the workers' dance two decades ago. And she'd kept on standing there, despite our hanky-panky by the Lake. Well, now she was leaving. With Sheppie. Without me. No more "Bunny, I need you." No "Bunny, let's go to the Lake." No "I love your hair, oh christ Bunny christ." No more "Hun-Bun, how about those papers?"

To hell with the both of you. I shook my head,

shaking Shep and Gladys out for good. Buh-bye.

Now, where to put the oak table? Simon would like it. Old Country oak, thick and solid to the point of stone. The forests here don't hold such trees. It wouldn't float, this table; it had a furniture heart. Furniture to the core, office furniture, dragged from the Old Country on a cargo liner by some ambitious Polack bossman, discarded from some congested second-story small-time manufacturer's office, picked up on the curb no doubt by some ardent young Colonist in the '30s, lugged into the back of someone's brother-in-law's truck, taken for a bumpy ride over the Bronx-Queens Expressway onto the even bumpier unpaved Colony roads, revived to serve as the center of every late-night meeting at the Barn, retired to have coffee served upon it in Gladys' living room, and now scheduled for yet another revival in my living room.

I could see the table waiting on heavy thick legs in Gladys' kitchen right now, ready to dig its clumsy heels into my thick blue carpet, the four small square indentations its legs would leave on my rug, failing to fade with the rest of the carpet. Even when I'm gone, when they take me away and throw me on the Chair, its footprints would remain. Maybe Simon could find some game in them, or devise a secret code out of the four dark squares, his fingers caressing the carpet pile. His fingers on my floor, touching the future marks from the legs of the soon-to-be-mine table. I knelt down on the floor, fingering the carpet the way he would.

Gladys came back in a rush in a truck. Her hands were moving even faster than her mouth, gesturing to and fro in a furious flurry, waving and slashing the air for emphasis on each word. Gladys the Nervous. Is she worried about leaving, or about me staying? Take a guess.

"Darling, thank god you're here. I'll have the boys move it into your living room before they load up my stuff. You could use a table in there, yes?"

I couldn't use a table, or anything else in my living room. I have never found a use for my living room. It's just glorified storage space, really. In Brooklyn, a second cousin would surely have been installed there by now. All that extra space, going to waste! Mama would be disgusted. But out here, where land is dirt cheap, dirt roads lead out to empty lots. Whole virgin woods stand unmolested; lakes and ponds lie unnamed, unowned. Houses grow big in the country. Even our little Colony bungalows have risen in the world, what with add-ons and rehabs, full of rooms where no one but the furniture sleeps.

The furniture, and Max's junk. Max was careful to distribute his possessions equally throughout the house. The living room got his books: heavy tomes on English common law, Spanish socialism, home carpentry.

Since he died, it's become something of an attic, my living room, where I junk up old *Daily Workers* and gardening tools. I wish I could say this is a widowish lapse on my part, the by-product of the lonely life, but the truth is, the living room started to accumulate junk from the moment we moved in. Max was no better than I at relaxing on the blue velvet couch. He tried; he hooked up a big old-fashioned floor radio in there, but never joined it. A living room, where we could really relax! What a luxury. After a couch, we'll get an end table, a bureau, some bookshelves. I remember buying the rug with the rest in mind. After a hard day of labor in the fields, a blue living room will be heaven to come home to, we told each other to justify such a bourgeois, non-collective treat.

But we only used it like an attic, junking it up with our nonsense. What a waste! As I cleared a space in the living room for the table, I felt an odd twinge of guilt.

"Careful, careful! What, you want to break all of Mrs. Edelman's china?" Gladys pummeled the two young boys with a string of admonishments as she followed them into the living room. "Ach, these Lewisboro boys, they think they're such big machers because they have a truck," she whispered loudly to me. "They'll be the death of me yet. We almost hit some kid as we backed out of my driveway! Not one of ours, at least. Some Lewisboro punk, no doubt. Now, out in Jersey, the kids don't run around in pickup trucks.

They have a basketball court right on our corner for them, and there's a Good Neighbor patrol around the..."

"What did he look like?" To even mention you to Gladys made me cringe.

"What did who look like?" She furrowed her brows and blinked, annoyed to be interrupted in her soliloquy on Jersey this, Jersey that.

"The boy. The kid you almost hit."

"Well for chrissakes, Sylvie, I don't know; like I said, he wasn't one of ours. But with these boys driving like maniacs, I wouldn't be surprised if some poor kid didn't get killed! And on these unpaved roads, well, I don't have to tell you. Now out in Teaneck, there's a speed limit that's strictly enforced."

"Did he have gray blue eyes?"

Gladys squinted at me. "Well, now that you mention it, yes, I believe he did. Goyishe eyes, like some little fershtinkener Black Shirt. Stared straight at me, he did. You getting friendly with the locals, eh Sylvie?"

Elitist. Class traitor. Stupid bitch. Despite her years leading the youth groups, singing fervent rounds of the "Internationale" and "Joe Hill" (she liked to harmonize), marching in Union Square proudly beside Shep, Gladys always was something of a snob.

Good riddance, I thought as I finally got her out of my house. "And say 'good-bye' to Sheppie for me," I said as innocently as I could as she walked down my driveway, up towards Danger Road, hopefully for the last time. "I'll miss you both, but I'm sure Sheppie'll be visiting me soon."

"Sure, sure, Sylvie," she sniffed, speeding up a bit. "Sure, sure." She always repeated herself like that when she was annoyed.

Closing the screen door, I laughed out loud, suddenly feeling triumphant. Buh-bye!

I cleaned my kitchen from top to bottom, cleaning Gladys' spittle off my marigold dishes, washing off her scent, Lily of the Valley and Lucky Strikes. Feh!

Outside, it was high noon. The hour of death, the

Romans believed, or so Mrs. Cohen taught us. I sprayed on some Evening of Paris. The sun glared, the tomatoes sweated.

I knew you were out there. I walked out into the garden. The tomatoes were turning purple, too much sun. Later, I thought. I'll water everyone later. Something, hmm, what is it now? Ah yes, the lemon smell.

Inside, I made some coffee and sat in the kitchen, drowsy.

And I found you.

*

The end.

*

What more can I tell you?
There's nothing more.

XXIX. If I've Told You Once, I've Told You Three Times

You can't scare me; I've seen that before.

The first time was on the Jersey farm, in the neighbor man's barn. They sent me to Jersey, I don't even know where; just somewhere in the green hills, to help out on someone's farm. A hungry mouth can always find food on a farm, my father reasoned. Papa had too many mouths already: four screaming kids and a sick wife, all living in two rooms on one workman's wages.

So I went. I wasn't upset; I was eight. What did I know? I loved the farm. The cows, the hay, the barn. One day I saw chickens, and knew that eggs were near. Papa was right: on a farm, a hungry mouth always does find food.

I didn't know the barn was our neighbor's; I didn't know about owning. I was eight. I was looking for eggs when the bullets hit, the roosting chicken spattering with blood redder than a cock's comb. I looked up, and there was a man, the neighbor man from the farm next to ours, cocking a shiny silver pistol at me.

"We shoot stray chickens," the neighbor-man grinned, and aimed straight at me. Only one chicken was hurt, but after that, I didn't play in his barn again.

The second time was at the shop. Mr. Lewin. He came up behind me, held the gun against my neck, a cold embrace, and grunted "Okay Sylvie, so you wanna go union? Do ya?" And let me go before I could answer, scuttling off and out the door, murmuring "Capitalist scum" under my breath. I don't remember what it looked like, but I still can feel it hard against my neck, a metal noose.

The last time was the charm. I saw it on the train. It was after.

I had a hunch that Simon was close, that if I took the right train, I could catch him.

It was fancy, new-fangled: short snout, bright silver, small handle. A streamlined version. I felt baggy and heavy beside it, suddenly aware of my shirt untucking out of my skirt.

It sat alone, in the seat across from me, unaccompanied by a body living or dead. The Lone Gun: there must be a radio show with such a title. I decided to sit beside it. Not to take, but to neighbor it.

When the train pulled into Grand Central, I left the gun sitting there, alone.

*

So this is the fourth. A large one, very nice.

But this is irrelevant. You want the rest of the story, even though you already know it. All right. Just for you, darling. The rest of the end, then. Why not?

0. Afterwards

I found his body. It was charred. It was a day old, by the looks of it. Bluish boils lumped the flesh, a gristly parody of teenage acne. His cheeks were roughened by...hair? I looked more closely. Yes, hair. I recognized its texture and color: the fuzzy beginnings of a beard.

Mickey Rooney! Goldenrod! Nebraska! Max!

I didn't yell.

*

Who killed him?

The hot wind. The sun. Short circuits. You. Hell, I don't know.

His feet were bare, scorched, the flesh puckering like it'd been in the bath too long. The toes were all curled under. He was missing an arm. And a finger, the left pinkie. The arm didn't bother me so much – it was a clean break – but the pinkie showed signs of struggle.

Below the waist he was still perfect. Cock sleeping on the right, nestling into the muscular thigh. Good night, legs. Everything still, everything the exact right shape, sloped and curved, even more perfectly placed now than before. The dog tag was twisted but intact.

"Simon," I said, wondering if he could still hear.

"Simon, Simon" I said, as if the word would flip the on-switch on.

"Simon," I cried, tears streaming down, everything blurred like it's raining.

-I.

Pissing your pants, are you? I'm not surprised. Pussy.

You reds always turn yellow. Sons of bitches. Raising your boys to be fairies and your cunts you stupid goddamn cunt to be pinko whores. I'll give you something to piss your pants about.

*

Oh, I'm not done with you. Cry all you want, cry your fucking eyes out, bleed the hell to death; I don't give a shit.

Just you wait for tomorrow. I got a chair custom-built for your fat ass, Sylvie, just waiting to fry you. Just you wait.

-II.

Tell me everything.

*

Come on, Mrs. Edelman. Sylvie.

*

We already know about the Barn, the Colony, the plot. Your husband Max was a known Communist. You are already a proven fellow-traveler at the very least.

We know all your secrets. What color your bathroom towels are (blue), what brand of coffee you drink (Maxwell House), your favorite snack (red licorice), your favorite radio show ("New and Views," 94.3 FM with that kike fellow-traveler Art Spellman.)

We already know the whole story, so you might as well just 'fess up. Maybe we'll let you off easy then.

Your sister told us everything. Poor Rose. Such a fine lady, stuck with a lousy pinko sister like you.

You wouldn't want anything to happen to Rose now, would you?

*

If you tell everything, and I mean everything, Mrs. E., you can get off with just a little red mark in your file and go live out in Jersey with Rose and Hesh. A fine couple, aren't they. *Real* Americans, not like these pinko creeps you got yourself mixed up with.

It doesn't matter; the boy told us everything.

*

Yes, I know I resemble him. We all do.

*

Why? That's none of your business, Mrs. E. I'll ask the questions here, if you don't mind.

He gave us all the nitty-gritty. What a sicko you are. How you like to suck. And not just cock: fingers, pinkies especially. You pathetic pervert commie freak. He told us every disgusting detail. How he pissed in your face. How you came with his toe in your mouth. Squealed like a bitch in heat. Commie pinko slut. Screwing a boy young enough to be your own grandson. Jesus.

You stink, Sylvia. "Mrs. Edelman." Hah. Fucking pinko whore. What would your poor husband think? Sylvia the Slut. He's probably rolling over in the grave right now.

We know everything. And anything we don't, we'll beat or fuck right out of you. And then fry your ass with a slice of bacon to cover the stench. We let you people in, opened the gates to all the goddamn kike scum like you, and what do we get? Traitors. Stinking commie kike pinko traitors, the lot of you.

We already know.

But we'll beat the rest of it out of you anyways, just to get all the sick details. Just for kicks. I'll do it myself. I have no problem hitting a girl. Not when she's a threat to my country. *My* country, Mrs. Edelman. Not yours anymore, you stupid traitor bitch.

We can take everything away. Take shit you didn't even know you had. And not just your commie crap, but everyone else's. Like Rose's house. Never thought of that when you were scheming away in that fucking commie den, did you? We can repossess it in a minute, infest it with termites, blow it up, a little kitchen incident, and no one will ever be the wiser. Or maybe we'll just take away the kids: Alfie, Stevie, and don't forget little Harry, grab them in their sleep. Rose wouldn't like that, now would she?

So that doesn't scare you? Sylvia? Mrs. E.?

*

You still won't talk? Come on, doll. Sheppie, Gladys, Louie, Joe: they've all finked on you already. What have you got to lose? What the fuck do you think you're protecting here exactly, Sylvia?

This is the U.S. of A., in case you've forgotten. We don't tolerate traitors like you, Mrs. Edelman. We'll burn down every last pinko joint and all the stinking kike commies inside to protect it. We didn't fight in double-ya double-ya two for a bunch of commies to overrun every goddamn school, every church, even a motherfucking cow town like Sylvan Lake, now did we? No siree. Right, Mrs. E.?

Christ. I should just kill you right now, not waste another stinking word on some old commie bag. Look at you. You're all sluts, too dirty to fuck. Wouldn't dirty my dick with a cow cunt like you.

Don't move. Did I say you could move? Did I? I ask you, *did I tell you to move*?

*

That hurts, now don't it, Mrs. E.?

Still got nothin' to say? Because there's lots more where that came from. Are you sure you have nothing to tell me? Because I'm sick of you. I been patient, but enough is enough. I've been a gentleman, but you sure haven't been no lady, now have you? Don't waste my time. Start talking.

-III.

For the last time, will you talk?

*

Okay, then. You asked for it.

*

Can't sit down now, can you? I'll break you but good. You know you're gonna break.

You're a patsy, Mrs. E. A patsy and a perv. Did you really think we'd tell you the truth about the boy? Animal, mineral, vegetable. Rat, runaway, pirate. Robot or boy. Traitor or angel. What's your guess?

*

You stupid little pinko bitch. You cocksucker.

*

Had enough yet? Fucking commie kike cow. Cocksucking commie bitch. I'll kick your ass from here to Moscow. I'll knock you up with some real American jism, not that commie piss you been sucking. You dirty whore.

*

Traitor.

*

Motherfucker.

*

Cunt.

-IV.

I sit here in the night, looking out of my cell into the dark of other cells. If I didn't know better, I'd think I was looking at my garden. I wouldn't be able to see much, because in the night, the vegetables are indistinct.

Are you still hidden there? Or in here?

No, if you were, I think I'd be able to see you, your eyes closed, your body naked and visible even in this final darkness.

I don't mind being here. It will be over soon.

It was a relief when it finally ended. Old Colony Road jammed with unmarked cars, a swarm of men inside, guns poised, listening. They should have shot me then. Yes, I would have preferred that. But the guns stayed tucked in their holsters, cuddling against each secret service leg.

So now I have to wait a bit longer. But that's okay; I'll watch the dark, and remember you however I want.

-V.

I watch the dark all night, seeing my garden.

In the morning as they take me away, I eat a tomato. My last request, no knife, all juice and hands and it's a bumper crop. Ha!

Jennifer Natalya Fink is a writer, children's bookmaker, teacher, hell-raiser, and Brooklynite. She has won a variety of awards for her fiction, including The Dana Award In The Novel, *STORY Magazine*'s Short Fiction Award, *The Georgetown Review*'s Fiction Award, and the Billy Heekin Foundation Award. She is the Founder and Gorilla-in-Chief of The Gorilla Press, a non-profit organization dedicated to promoting literacy through bookmaking.